Newcastle
City

Ne

Du

. . . .

. . . .

. . . . . .

. . . . . .

. . . .

. .

. . . .

. . .

. .

. . . .

. . . .

. . . . . .

Pleas
sho

"You scare the hell out of me, Clara."

It should have driven them apart and broken the spell, but it did exactly the opposite. The air felt warmer and the interior of the car smaller as she watched his tongue wet his lips.

"Me? Scare you?" Her words came out on a squeak.

"I don't know how to act around you. You're different. You've been through stuff I can't understand. I never know if I'm going to make things better or create a disaster. If I mess up or do something wrong, remember I'm trying to do the right thing."

"The right thing?" she echoed.

He nodded slowly. "Yes. The right thing." He sighed. "I'm trying to do the right thing for everybody, so I'm bound to screw it up somehow."

Clara fought the urge to reach over and touch his thigh. He was being terribly open, wasn't he? She was starting to realize that beneath the sexy rebel was someone who cared very deeply. Who was kind.

Which made him an even worse sort of trouble.

Dear Reader,

'All the heroes have not gone. There are many undiscovered heroes left. They are disguised as everyday men and women who touch our lives and help us to be better.'

My sister-in-law Julie wrote those words in her eulogy to her dad—my father-in-law—who passed away while I was writing this book. As we sat in the kitchen and typed it up I got to that part and totally choked up. Part of it was acknowledging the men in the family I married into—strong men, who believe in working hard and loving big. Another part was simply believing in those words. *All the heroes have not gone.* That is, after all, why I love writing romance.

I think those words were partially responsible for how this story turned out, because Tyson ended up being different than I initially imagined. I would expect him to do one thing and he'd turn around and surprise me with a tender side I didn't know he had. I discovered he knew how to be gentle. That he cared very deeply about his family, had his own insecurities, and a gigantic sense of honour. Turns out my rebellious hero ended up having a heart of gold.

Heroism comes in many forms. It is standing up for someone, or simply standing beside them as they face their demons. It is honouring a commitment, doing the right thing even when it hurts, or pitching in and lending a hand in a time of need.

Heroes are all around us—all we have to do is look.

And sometimes remember.

Warmest wishes

Donna

Don't miss the first book
in the *Cadence Creek Cowboys* duet
THE LAST REAL COWBOY
April 2012
**Available in eBook format
from www.millsandboon.co.uk**

THE REBEL RANCHER

BY
DONNA ALWARD

MILLS & BOON

First published in Great Britain 2012
by Mills & Boon, an imprint of Harlequin (UK) Limited.
Harlequin (UK) Limited, Eton House, 18-24 Paradise Road,
Richmond, Surrey TW9 1SR

© Donna Alward 2012

ISBN: 978 0 263 22760 4

Harlequin's policy is to use papers that are natural, renewable and recyclable products and made from wood grown in sustainable forests. The logging and manufacturing processes conform to the legal environmental regulations of the country of origin.

Printed and bound in Great Britain
by CPI Antony Rowe, Chippenham, Wiltshire

A busy wife and mother of three (two daughters and the family dog), **Donna Alward** believes hers is the best job in the world: a combination of stay-at-home mum and romance novelist. An avid reader since childhood, Donna always made up her own stories. She completed her Arts Degree in English Literature in 1994, but it wasn't until 2001 that she penned her first full-length novel and found herself hooked on writing romance. In 2006 she sold her first manuscript, and now writes warm, emotional stories for the Mills & Boon® Cherish™ line.

In her new home office in Nova Scotia, Donna loves being back on the east coast of Canada after nearly twelve years in Alberta, where her career began, writing about cowboys and the west. Donna's debut romance, HIRED BY THE COWBOY, was awarded the Booksellers Best Award in 2008 for Best Traditional Romance.

With the Atlantic Ocean only minutes from her doorstep, Donna has found a fresh take on life and promises even more great romances in the near future!

Donna loves to hear from readers. You can contact her through her website at www.donnaalward.com, her page at www.myspace.com/dalward, or through her publisher.

Recent titles by the same author:

THE LAST REAL COWBOY
HOW A COWBOY STOLE HER HEART
A FAMILY FOR THE RUGGED RANCHER
HONEYMOON WITH THE RANCHER

**These books are also available in eBook format
from www.millsandboon.co.uk**

To Darrell. You're the glue, and I love you for it
and
To Ralph 1940–2011

CHAPTER ONE

CLARA HAD HEARD A LOT about Tyson Diamond. Some of it good, a lot of it questionable. But none of the reports had warned her that he was over six feet of sexy cowboy with a break-your-heart smile and a devilish gleam in his eye.

And now he was striding this way as Angela, still resplendent in her wedding dress, waved him over.

Clara wondered if she could say her final congratulations to Sam and Angela and escape before Tyson reached them. She'd managed to avoid him up to this point, after all. She'd been helping his father, Virgil, with his rehab after his stroke, and her off-duty hours were spent helping Angela plan the wedding from the safety of Butterfly House, the transition shelter Angela managed and where Clara currently lived. And Ty had been wrapping up his business up north and spending time with Sam as they worked together running the ranch. Somehow she and Tyson had failed to cross paths in the weeks leading up to the wedding.

Until today.

This afternoon he'd turned up spit-polished in his black suit with his hair just a little messy. Her mouth had gone dry just looking at him. Ty was exactly the sort of man she tried to avoid. Tall, sexy, confident and careless. The kind that ate shy girls like her for breakfast. The kind that girls like her could never resist.

Her heart had taken a little jump and she'd caught her breath before she could even put a thought together. But Ty had sauntered in, all long legs and crooked grins, and there it had been. Whomp. Attraction, pure and simple. Nothing in the world could have surprised her more.

He was still several feet away but closing the gap fast, and Clara felt panic start to bubble, making her chest cramp and her breath shorten. She wasn't ready to handle this. She felt as tongue-tied as a schoolgirl only with the sobering wisdom of a woman who'd been through hell. Putting the two together only created chaos in her mind. A quick exit was in order. She turned to Sam and Angela and forced a smile.

"I'm going to take Virgil in now, but I wanted to say happy wedding day to you both." She gave Angela a brief hug. "I'm going to miss you around the house, but you're going to have a wonderful time on your honeymoon."

Sam hugged Clara as well. She didn't feel the unholy urge to pull away and run the way she usually did when faced with someone intruding on her personal space. She'd learned to trust Sam in the weeks leading up to the wedding, especially after he'd stood beside Angela as she faced her own demons.

"You did great today," he said quietly, giving her arm a gentle squeeze. "And you look beautiful."

Heat infused her cheeks at the compliment and at the knowledge that Tyson was nearly upon their little group. "Thank you. Now I'd better get Virgil inside, he was looking tired…."

Sam's voice cut her off as he looked over her shoulder. "Have you met Ty yet?" he asked. "Ty, this is Clara Ferguson, Dad's nurse. You'll be seeing a lot of each other from now on."

Too late. Clara closed her eyes and took a steady breath. She really wished she wasn't blushing as she turned around, but she could feel the heat centered in her cheeks. Dammit.

Tyson's jaw sported a faint shadow of stubble and the suit coat hung awkwardly on his rangy frame. But the style worked for him and his dark eyes held a gleam of approval as he looked down at her. His appraising gaze made something curl inside her uncomfortably. What she wouldn't give for a pair of comfy jeans and a baggy sweater right about now. The sage-green bridesmaid's dress was far too fitted to her figure and made her feel conspicuous. Compliments were well and good, but she was far more confident when she was in her comfort zone.

"Mr. Diamond," she said, setting her jaw defiantly as she held out her hand. She could set the tone between them right here and now. Businesslike—exactly the way it should be between her and Virgil's adopted son.

But it was an utter flop of an attempt. His warm fingers enveloped hers in a strong, lingering grip. A hint of a smile flirted with the corners of his mouth. "It's just Ty," he replied, with a voice as smooth and chocolaty as the dark depths of his eyes. "Or Tyson if I'm on your bad side."

Bad side? Right now she felt as though she might swallow her tongue as she looked into his face. She *liked* the feel of her hand in his. Where was the old reliable revulsion she'd become accustomed to? The instinctive need to pull away and keep her distance? She knew how to deal with that. This was all new territory, and she was momentarily at a loss for words.

His smile widened and she pulled her hand away, hiding her fingers within the clasp of her left hand. "Right," she said, her voice shaking. "Well, I'd better get your dad inside. Good night, everyone."

She couldn't meet his gaze as she scuttled away, but she heard Sam's voice and it made her burn with humiliation.

"Go easy," Sam warned Ty.

"Did I do anything?" There was a hint of defensiveness in Ty's voice that fit with what she'd heard through the grapevine. That things weren't as smooth sailing between the brothers as they seemed.

She quickened her steps so she wouldn't hear Sam's answer. Everything she'd heard around town was right, then. She hadn't been able to tune out the snatches of conversation that had reached her ears today. The return of the prodigal Tyson was a hot topic. Unfortunately so was his track record with the ladies.

Tyson Diamond was gorgeous and he knew it. He was also a wild card and Sam's illegitimate cousin who'd been adopted by Virgil and Molly as a baby. *Trouble.* He was the last person who should make Clara blush and stammer. She was smarter than that, wasn't she?

Now he'd hung up his rodeo spurs and was coming home to run the ranch with Sam. With Virgil still recovering and needing regular care, they were going to see each other *all the time*.

Great. Just wonderful.

Clara helped Virgil get settled, but once she was alone in the quiet house her unease came back with a vengeance, sending tingles shooting up the backs of her legs and making an all-too-familiar weight settle in her chest. It had been a long, tiring day and her defenses were down. That had to be the reason why Ty's simple handshake had made her react in such an uncharacteristic way. Or maybe it was just weddings. Weddings did tend to make people sentimental and romantic, right? She twisted her fingers. Or stupid.

Either way, it was *one day*. It didn't matter a bit if she found Tyson attractive. She had no interest in romance. Not after all that had been taken away from her in the name of "love." She had her eye set on her goal and nothing was going to divert her from it.

She escaped into the first-floor powder room, sat down on the closed toilet and focused on breathing deeply for a few minutes. Once she'd regrouped she got up, ran some cold water over her hands and carefully touched them to her cheeks, soothing the heat there without marring her makeup. She could do this. She'd come too far to go back to hiding away at the first whiff of discomfort. Goodness, a year ago she would never have made it through a day like today. She shouldn't let something like this rattle her.

She stared into the mirror. "Living in fear is not living. I will not live in fear."

The words soothed, both from sentiment and habit. She let out a breath and straightened her shoulders. She opened the door and nearly ran straight into Tyson's chest.

His hands gripped her arms, steadying her from toppling over in the heels she wasn't used to wearing.

"Whoa," he said, his low voice rippling over her nerve endings.

Her faced flamed anew, his word choice making her feel decidedly klutzy and horsy. And he was touching her again. "I'm sorry," she stammered. "I didn't know anyone was waiting for the bathroom."

"I was waiting for *you*," he replied easily. He squatted down slightly so that he was closer to her height and peered into her face. She didn't like the way he was looking at her. As though he was trying to figure her out. The less he knew about her the better. And she planned to keep it that way, no matter how often their paths crossed in the coming weeks.

"Waiting for me?"

"You ran off quite a while ago. I wanted to be sure you're all right."

"Of course I am." His hands seemed to burn through the soft fabric of her dress to the skin beneath. She conjured up the polite smile she'd practiced all week in the mirror. "It took me a while to get your dad settled, that's all."

Liar, her brain protested, but she ignored it. A warmth ran through her at his concern. Usually she managed to fly under the radar, blending into her surroundings like a chameleon. People usually didn't notice if she came or went. But Ty had.

Despite her assurances, Tyson didn't budge from blocking the hallway. His lips curled up in the most alluring manner. Lordy, with a smile like that she bet he didn't even have to try with the ladies. They'd all fall in his lap, wouldn't they?

She stepped around him and he dropped his fingers from her arms. She breathed a little easier once he wasn't touching her anymore. "If you'll excuse me…"

"What's your hurry?" he asked, his soft voice humming over her already raw nerves, making her pause, making her realize once more that they were very alone here in the house while the party went on outside.

"I should get back to Angela, make sure…"

"Angela and Sam have gone. You missed the throwing of the bouquet."

Clara's heart sank. Had she truly been gone so very long? Not that she'd wanted to catch the bouquet by any means, but she'd disappeared into a corner exactly the way she'd promised herself she wouldn't. Once again she'd missed out on good things because she was too busy hiding herself away from something awkward or uncomfortable.

"I thought all the single women fought over catching it." He raised his eyebrows. "You *are* single, aren't you?"

The question was so ludicrous that Clara almost laughed. Single? Absolutely. For now and forever.

"I'm not interested in catching any bouquets," she remarked, finally looking up in his eyes. They were good eyes, she had to admit. They were dark brown but she noticed now that they had little golden flecks around the pupils and crinkles in the corners. His lips were finely shaped, full where they needed to be full and just now curved in what she was realizing was his trademark smile—tilted to one side as if he was sharing a joke. All in all it was a bit lethal, and he was just the sort of man she might have been interested in before.

Before. She looked away from Ty's handsome face and focused on the closet door behind his shoulder. It seemed her life was split into two distinct parts. Before Jackson and after Jackson. The carefree Clara she had been before no longer existed. Jackson had destroyed her.

For well over a year she'd been rebuilding herself from square one. The new Clara stood here now, in a new life and with a new job. She had to remember that. She had accomplished so much. She was a lot more careful now. A lot more cautious. A lot smarter.

"That's a shame," Ty responded, and she heard a laugh in his voice. "Because I caught this."

She caught a glimpse of a blue-and-white lace garter as he stretched it out over a finger. Was he flirting with her? It seemed preposterous. She was plain as ditch water, and to a man like Ty, probably twice as dull. For heaven's sake, she lived in a women's shelter and spent her days as a private nurse. She was distinctly unworldly and unexciting. And Ty was a rodeo star and drifter. They had absolutely nothing in common.

She was therefore surprised to find that she didn't feel particularly threatened by his presence. Ty Diamond was dangerous, all right. A real bad boy from all accounts. Yet somehow she felt…safe.

"Lucky you," she replied dryly, proud that she'd managed to keep her tongue from tying in knots and trying to summon what used to be, in the *before Jackson* days, a ready sense of humor. "Do you have a girl in mind? Tradition says you'll be the next bachelor to be married." She smiled, but it felt forced, like she was baring her teeth. "Who caught the bouquet? A likely candidate for the next Mrs. Diamond, perhaps?"

"Amy Wilson, and I hardly think so."

His displeasure was so obvious Clara let out a half laugh, half gasp. She was familiar with Amy's vivacious and gossipy ways. Amy had had plenty to say about Tyson today and little of it good. It had sounded a bit like sour grapes. "That's not very nice."

He shrugged. "Amy and I have never seen eye to eye. She wanted Sam, you know. And when she saw me catch the garter she hightailed it to the other side of the garden, well out of my reach."

"Why?" She looked up and saw he was still smiling that sexy half smile and she bit down on her lip. "I mean, why doesn't Amy like you?" She couldn't imagine being repulsed by Ty. He might look slightly out of place in formal wear, but it didn't disguise the fact that he was a stunning display of masculinity. Gorgeous enough even to fluster her—someone who'd been immune to any sort of charms for some time now. The new Clara was far too practical to be distracted.

He stepped back. "Easy. The adopted bastard doesn't have the same shine as the heir apparent."

Clara turned away and began walking back to the kitchen so they would be out of the close confines of the hall. The words had been said flippantly, but he hadn't quite been able to disguise the bitterness behind them.

"Did you say that just to shock me?"

In the kitchen, Ty went to the fridge and took out a beer, popping the top as he leaned his hips against the counter. "If I said no, would you believe me?" He took a drink.

She watched him for a few seconds. He wanted her to think he'd been joking but she saw something behind his eyes. Hurt. She was more sensitive to that sort of thing after what she'd been through. All she knew about Ty was that he was really Sam's cousin, and Virgil and Molly had adopted him. What had it been like, growing up at Diamondback, in Sam's shadow? Being a Diamond but still knowing that he didn't quite belong? She found the Diamond house with all its expensive trappings a bit intimidating. Had Ty? Was that why he'd left?

"I don't think I would believe you," she said. "I think you might just enjoy shocking people."

His eyebrow came up and his grin flashed. "You could be right, Clara."

There was something intimate about the way he said her name. Her pulse began to hammer again. How did he do that?

He gestured with his bottle, a careless flick of the wrist. "So, what *would* it take to shock you?"

She swallowed. She might be practical but she understood a come-on when she heard it. Ty hadn't moved an inch but he suddenly seemed much closer. She replayed the conversation she'd heard today to center her thoughts.

Ty Diamond is a flirt and a player, the woman had said. *It's as natural to him as breathing.*

Clara knew she was nothing special. And if this was Tyson's way of making this a game, she wasn't playing. She met his gaze and raised a single eyebrow. "That won't work with me."

He laughed. "You're tougher than you look. Well, here we are anyway, both avoiding all the wedding hoopla. Get you something to drink?"

She shook her head, a bit surprised he seemed to brush off her comment like it was nothing. And he'd called her tough. He probably had no idea how much of a compliment that was. "If Sam and Angela have gone, I should probably be getting home."

Ty leaned a hip against the counter. "To Butterfly House, right?"

She nodded. It was no secret where she lived, but she didn't quite like Ty knowing, for some reason. His dark eyes assessed her a little too closely until she felt like a bug under a microscope. She momentarily wondered if Angela had sent Tyson in on purpose to make sure she wasn't alone. While she appreciated the sentiment, lately she'd found herself chafing against the constant analysis of her every move and thought. Sometimes she just wanted to get on with her life rather than dissect it to pieces.

"Whatever you're thinking, just ask, Tyson. Don't try to guess. And don't stare at me. It makes me uncomfortable." She was learning to stand up for herself, to set her own boundaries, but even so a quiver of anxiety always followed such a demonstration of self-assurance. It was hard to get past the "don't rock the boat" mentality.

"I didn't mean to stare." His gaze softened. "Angela told me you are a...is *client* the right word?"

"It works." Her heart started drumming all over again,

and not in the glorious anticipatory way it had before. He was going to ask. People always got curious when they found out she lived at the shelter, like they were somehow entitled to her story and the sordid details. "Is that why you followed me inside? To get the details?"

He put the beer bottle down on the countertop. He'd undone his tie and the black silk hanging against the brilliant white of his shirt made him seem approachable. Touchable. Not for her, though. He probably had a string of buckle bunnies clear down to Texas. A man like Tyson Diamond would eat her alive and spit out the bones before moving on to the next conquest.

She felt a tiny stab in her heart, remembering how she'd fallen for Jackson only to discover the true man underneath after it was too late. Too late for so many things. Her throat tightened as she grieved for all that she'd lost. Jackson had been handsome and charming, too. In the beginning.

Angela had talked to her about not judging every man by the abuser's yardstick, and in her head Clara knew she was right. Her heart was still a little too bruised, though, to trust her judgment completely. She was perfectly happy going along the way she was. It would be even better when she was completely independent. She couldn't wait to be one hundred percent in charge of her own life.

"You looked panicked out there. I know the feeling, and I wanted to make sure you were okay, that's all."

He wasn't asking about her past. And he was telling the truth. His words were utterly sincere.

"You don't strike me as the panic type," she responded, getting a glass from the cupboard and filling it with water.

"I'm okay—in my element," he responded smoothly. "Garden weddings? Not so much my element. Neither is this monkey suit."

"I imagine you are more of a jeans and boots kind of guy."

"Definitely," he answered. "Anyway, back to my original question. Are you sure you're okay?"

"Of course I am," she replied.

"Okay," he said, sticking his hands in his trouser pockets, making his suit jacket flare away from his hips in a most attractive way. Clara swallowed. She remembered not two months ago, asking Angela about Sam as he chopped wood in the back yard at Butterfly House. She had told Angela there was a big difference between appreciating the package and taking the leap into something more. She'd looked at Sam through the window that day and found him handsome. But Ty...Ty resembled Sam but with an added something she couldn't put her finger on. For the first time since crawling away from Jackson, battered and bruised, she was definitely appreciating the package, all wrapped up in a suit and patent shoes.

Her tongue snuck out to wet her lips and she saw Ty's gaze follow the movement. All the air seemed to go out of the room.

She fought to be rational. Other than his hands briefly on her arms as she came barreling out of the bathroom, he hadn't touched her or made any sort of suggestion that he was interested.

Except...

Except for the dark gleam in his eyes as he stared at her lips. There was just this *thing* hovering around them. It had been a long time since she'd felt it, but it was like riding a bike. Once you experienced it once, it came back to you in a flash—whether you wanted it to or not. Now she found herself staring at his lips and wondering what it would be like to be kissed.

Reality hit like a splash of cold water. "I really should

go," she said, taking a step backwards. Her voice sounded higher than normal and she swallowed. "Your mother will be expecting me here on time tomorrow. Weddings are all well and good, but real life has a tendency to intrude, and your dad has physio in the morning. It was nice meeting you, Ty."

"You're not going to stay for a dance or two?"

"God, no."

The answer came so quickly and with such force that she didn't have time to think about *not* saying it. There was acknowledging the presence of some sort of...*chemistry,* she supposed was a good word for it. But dancing—touching—in front of people? She swallowed. Her progress hadn't quite extended that far. She'd even said no to Sam—who she trusted more than she'd trusted any man since leaving her ex—when he asked for a dance. He'd been perfectly understanding, but she'd stood by the sidelines watching everyone else dance, feeling silly. Like a coward.

Ty's gaze darkened until it was almost black, and she felt his cool withdrawal. Leaving the half-full bottle, he headed towards the deck doors, stopping for just a moment beside her. She could feel the heat from his body and the crisp scent of whatever aftershave he wore surrounded her in a cloud of masculinity. "Miss Ferguson." He nodded, then continued on his way. The click of the French door let her know that he was gone in a swell of country music that was immediately muted; she couldn't bear to turn around and watch him stride away.

She hadn't meant it how it sounded. She'd only been thinking of the idea of being held close in a man's arms. The very prospect was laughable. Dancing was so intimate. The one thing she still hadn't managed to shake in all the therapy sessions and the time that had passed was her aversion to having her personal space invaded. She hadn't been held by a man since walking away. It triggered too many memories of how Jackson had held her and told her he loved her, only to turn around and use those same loving hands to...

She shuddered. But she knew how it must have sounded to Ty. It had been an indirect invitation on his part and she'd refused before he'd been able to take a breath. Right after he'd called himself the adopted bastard. He'd looked at her lips and she'd acted like she was repulsed.

He would think she considered herself just like Amy—a cut above. But he was wrong, so very wrong.

Tomorrow she'd have to face him. He was living here now, and she would be here every day, helping Molly with the household chores and putting Virgil through his physio exercises. It would be incredibly awkward at best if they left things the way they were now. She should at least explain that it wasn't him, right?

She rolled her shoulders back and resolved that she would not have an anxiety attack in the next fifteen minutes. Instead she would take another step towards having a normal life. She couldn't lean on Angela and Sam any longer. "Living in fear is not living," she repeated to the empty room. Wasn't it about time she started putting that mantra into practice? Wasn't it time she did something about the one thing that still held her back?

Her hand tightened on the handle of the French door. She'd be able to face herself—and Tyson Diamond—in the morning.

It was time to move on.

CHAPTER TWO

TYSON PULLED THE TIE from around his neck and rammed it into his pocket. The fall evening was cool and twilight was setting in. White solar minilights were twisted around the garden poplars creating a fairy glow, and chafing dishes held the last remnants of the wedding feast. This was so not his scene. He'd far rather be enjoying a steak in a comfortable pair of jeans. But he'd promised Sam to see out the day and he'd do it.

He hadn't expected the sudden hit to his pride just now, though. He hadn't even had the chance to actually ask Clara to dance before she'd flat-out refused. For the first time in as long as he could remember, his charm had let him down. It was humbling to a man who'd spent a good amount of his youth perfecting his way around women, and with a consistent rate of success. Riding bulls and charming cowgirls was what he'd done best.

And Clara Ferguson had seen right through his act.

He shouldn't take it personally, he knew that. Not considering her past. But he did just the same. The same way he did whenever someone slapped him on the back but offered Sam their hand. Always second-best. Not that Sam had ever bought into the idea. He'd always insisted by word and deed that they were equal brothers.

Oh, he knew there were people who thought that there

was some weird sibling rivalry thing between them, but they were wrong. It was why Ty was willing to come back now. For Sam. And deep down, for his dad, too. Virgil had always picked apart every single thing Tyson ever did. He'd never understood that Tyson loved this ranch as much as Sam did. Trying to get the old man's approval had been killing him, so he'd ventured out on his own years ago to save his sanity. To avoid saying things he might always regret.

Now he was back and already feeling suffocated. But it was time to stop running away. Time to take his place in the family—whether the old man liked it or not.

He frowned and checked his watch. He'd give it ten minutes, and then he was taking his dented pride and packing it in. Tomorrow the real work began—Sam would be gone on his honeymoon, and the day-to-day running of Diamondback would be left to Ty. He was looking forward to the work.

The butting of heads with his dad would start, too, he imagined. He rolled his shoulders, willing out the tension. Virgil had hardly spoken to him since his return two days ago, other than a few grunts and disparaging comments that Ty had, for the most part, ignored, more out of consideration for his mother, Molly, than anything else. Ty knew very well that their father thought that Sam could do no wrong and it was a big mistake to give Ty equal say in running the ranch. He was a damn sight smarter than his father gave him credit for. He always had been. And he intended to prove it. He had ideas. But first he needed to assess the operation and make a plan. Virgil considered Tyson unreliable, but Tyson knew all about calculating risks. He'd been doing it for years.

The hired band whipped the crowd into a frenzy with a

fast-paced polka, and Ty checked his watch again—only a minute had passed.

It had been a mistake to go after Clara. He'd been way-laid by the bouquet and garter catching, but when he'd gone in the house and realized she was locked in the bath-room he'd been alarmed. He knew what Butterfly House was about. He'd felt her fingers tremble in his when they shook hands and had been automatically transported to a day three years ago when he'd interrupted a "situation."

All he'd wanted to do was reassure her that Diamond-back was a safe place…and then she'd run into him, he'd put his hands on her and everything he'd planned to say evaporated. The shocking thing was for a moment he'd thought she'd felt it, too, when the air hummed between them in the kitchen.

It wasn't the first time he'd been wrong.

The music changed and a movement caught his eye. Clara, in her sage-colored dress, tugging a shawl closer around her shoulders against the fall chill. She'd be leav-ing now, then, he thought, and scowled. He'd been an ass, trying to flirt with her. He hadn't mastered the art of polite chit chat and other social graces. Until tonight, they hadn't been required. How did a guy talk to a woman who was in a situation like hers, anyway? He did the only thing he knew how—and came off looking like an idiot. What had he been thinking, asking her to dance?

Clara didn't go around the house to where the cars were parked. Instead she crossed the grass towards the crowd. She looked up and around the throng until she met his eyes and her gaze stopped roaming. His heart gave a sharp kick in response—a surprise. Frightened girls with innocent eyes were so not his type. He was more into confident women who hung around waiting for the bull riders with the big belt buckles. Girls who were only in it for their own eight seconds and no further commitments.

There were at least a dozen reasons why he should stay clear of Clara Ferguson. He could list three off the top without blinking: she had too much baggage, she worked for the family and he'd only cause her trouble.

But she kept coming, her glossy walnut curls twisting over her shoulders like silk ribbons. The cut of her dress was simple and quite conservative, skimming down her figure and showing her curves without revealing much skin. The effect was sexier than it should have been, he realized. She was nothing like the women he dated. Maybe that was why he was noticing her today, but this was as far as it would go. Noticing. And he didn't even need Sam's earlier warning to tell him so.

She stopped in front of him and her chest rose as she took a deep breath. He realized he was holding his and slowly let it out. "Clara?"

She gave him a smile so sweet, so fragile, that it frightened the hell out of him.

"Would you like to dance, Tyson?"

A good puff of air could probably have knocked him over. He stared at her for a good five seconds until her smile began to waver and uncertainty clouded her dark blue eyes. He wasn't sure why, but something had prompted her to change her mind, and he sensed it had taken a lot of courage for her to come out here and ask.

So what was he supposed to do now? She'd been very clear about not wanting to dance—particularly with him. She'd pulled away from him twice now, and if they danced he'd have to touch her. In several places. Odd, but that thought fired his blood more than anything—or anyone—had in weeks.

But he got the feeling that if he declined it would be

about more than refusing a simple turn on the floor. "I thought you didn't want to dance."

She lifted her chin. "I changed my mind. But if you don't want to, that's fine." She started to turn away.

"I didn't say that." Hell, he might have blown it the first time, but she was here now, right? Something had brought her back out here tonight.

She paused, looked over her shoulder at him. Like she wanted him to believe she was in control. He knew better. She had no idea what she was doing. He should walk away right now—it would be better for them both. This whole day had him out of his comfort zone, and Clara was waiting with her sweet, sad eyes for his answer.

He held out his hand and waited. Just because he wasn't a gentleman ninety percent of the time didn't mean he couldn't fake it.

She put her hand in his and he felt the tremor against his palm. Hell. He was not good at this sort of thing. He was used to a not-so-subtle pressing of bodies on the dance floor. An invitation and a promise of things to come. Clara wasn't like that, was she? She was as flighty as a scared rabbit. Innocent.

Ty led her to the dance "floor"—an expanse of even ground in front of the band. As a waltz began, he put his right hand along the warm curve of her waist and clasped her fingers lightly in his left. He had no idea how close to get or if he should say something or… A cold sweat broke out at the back of his neck. Wasn't it hysterical that a man like him was suddenly so unsure what to do?

She'd gone quite pale, so he let go of her waist and put a finger beneath her chin.

Her last partner had abused her—Sam had said as much when he'd issued the warning to tread carefully. Now, as she tensed beneath his chaste touch, he felt an immediate,

blinding hatred for the man who had damaged such a beautiful creature, followed by something unfamiliar and un-
settling as he realized he was feeling unusually protective.

He lifted her chin with his finger and said simply, "You
make the rules."

Emotions flooded her eyes—what he thought was gratitude and relief and maybe even a touch of fear. He was
not a particularly good man, and he was certainly not
good enough for her, but he wasn't cruel or oblivious. So
he waited for her to clasp his hand in hers again before
he made his feet move, taking her with him around the
dirt floor, making sure there was lots of space between
their bodies.

They made small steps around the dance area, neither
speaking, but Ty felt the moment she finally began to relax
in his arms. He wanted to pull her closer, to nestle her in
the curves of his body, feel her softness against him, but
he kept a safe distance, honoring his word to let her take
the lead. Clara wasn't like other women. There were different rules to be followed. Hell, usually there were no rules.

The first song finished and led straight into another.
There was only a pause in their steps and then, by some
sort of unspoken agreement, they moved as one again,
swaying gently to the music. Her breasts brushed against
his jacket, an innocent whisper of contact that he normally
wouldn't notice but right now sent his blood racing. Her
temple rested lightly against his chin and the floral scent
of her shampoo filled his nostrils. There was something
inherently sweet about Clara, and he did not normally have
a sweet tooth when it came to women. But he couldn't deny
that what he was feeling was attraction. Arousal. As the
fiddle scraped in the background, his lips nuzzled against
the soft hair at her temple and his eyes closed, drawing in

her scent that reminded him of his mother's lily of the valley. Her skin was warm and soft and tasted like summer.

The song ended and Ty stepped back, shaken.

But worse than that was looking down at Clara and seeing her eyes swimming with tears. A quick survey showed him that several people were watching them curiously, and why not? It was no secret that Clara was a resident at the women's shelter, and Ty knew his reputation—quite intentional when all was said and done. The cocky, confident rebel image was a lot easier to maintain than the truth, after all.

But Clara didn't deserve gossip or prying eyes. To his dismay a tear slipped out of the corner of her eye and down her cheek.

"Let's get you away from here," he murmured, squeezing her hand, feeling instantly sorry he'd let things go as far as they had during the dance. In another time, another place, with another woman, that sort of soft kiss would have been nothing. But here he'd forgotten himself. The best he could do now was get her away from the gossip.

Her eyes widened at his suggestion. "Away...as in?" He watched as she swallowed.

"Away from busybodies," he said quietly. "I promise you, Clara, you don't have to be afraid of me. I won't hurt you."

She pulled her hand out of his and her face paled. She seemed oblivious to the inquisitive stares of the wedding guests as she stumbled backwards.

"I've heard that before." The words sounded jerked from her throat, harsh and disjointed. "This was a mistake. A horrible, horrible mistake."

She turned on her heel and ran off, dashing out of the garden as she rushed to the house. Her shawl fluttered out of the crook of her arm and settled on the grass. Ty was left standing in the middle of the dance area feeling like a first-class fool.

He walked over to where her shawl lay on the cool grass and picked it up, running the soft fabric through his fingers.

He'd spooked her big-time. It was probably just as well when all was said and done. But now he had an additional reason he wished he hadn't promised Molly he'd move back into the ranch house. He wasn't sure what would be worse—the awkwardness with Clara or the antagonism between him and his father.

She was afraid of him.

The next few months were going to be hell.

Clara kneaded the biscuit dough with a bit more force than necessary, flattening it on the countertop before rolling it and pushing the heels of her hands against it again. She'd put Virgil through his physio exercises already and he'd fallen asleep over his crossword puzzle, tired from the exertions and from all the excitement of the previous day. She'd changed his bedding after his bath, given him his meds and made sure he was comfortable in his favorite chair. Molly was out at a church women's breakfast. And Ty was…

Ty was out in the barns somewhere. Thank goodness.

Just the thought of Tyson made her cheeks grow hot. The few times they'd crossed paths in the days since the wedding, he'd offered a polite greeting and moved on, barely meeting her eyes. And who could blame him? She'd cried, for Pete's sake, and run off. For someone who wasn't into drama or making a spectacle, she'd indulged in plenty. No wonder he kept his distance from her now. Her intentions to smooth the way had been a big fat failure.

Then again, he never should have kissed her either. Even if it hadn't been technically a kiss.

She flipped the dough and kneaded it again, welcoming the rhythmic motion. It was almost therapeutic the way her arm muscles moved and flexed as she pushed the dough around the board. She tended to cook when she needed to empty her mind. And her mind was plenty full.

But so far it wasn't working. Things around the Diamond place were tense. Ty complicated matters—and not just for her. Virgil had been irritable lately, growling at her during his exercises and wearing a scowl more often than a smile. She had half a mind to sit the both of them down and tell them to talk rather than stomp around beating their chests. There was clearly some sort of power struggle at work and it wasn't good for Virgil. It wasn't her place to say anything, though. And sheer embarrassment kept her from offering Ty more than a quiet hello.

She'd fallen quite under his spell while dancing. Their bodies had been touching. Her hands paused over the dough for a minute, remembering. On one hand, it had been a stunning victory over her personal-space phobia. But it had also been a huge mistake. Come on—Ty Diamond? And it had been in front of half of Cadence Creek. She gave her head a shake.

She employed the rolling pin next, rolling the dough out exactly half an inch thick. The more Ty stayed out of her way the better. Virgil needed to stay focused on his rehabilitation, and Ty made Clara feel…

Well, that was the problem, wasn't it? He made Clara feel, full stop. She'd gotten as caught up as any other woman in the romance of the wedding, wooed by the adoring looks Sam and Angela shared, the soft music, the beautiful flowers and pretty dresses. That was the only explanation that made any sense at all.

Clara applied the cookie cutter to the dough with a vengeance, cutting circles and plopping them on a cookie sheet. In the clear light of day she realized he had felt sorry for her. That stung, but she should have retained a little dignity rather than fleeing. She had no one to blame but herself.

She heard the front door shut. Molly couldn't be back already, Sam and Angela were going to be in Ottawa on their honeymoon for another week, and no one else would walk in without knocking. That left Ty. Speak of the devil.

"Morning," he said, coming through to the kitchen in his socked feet. Buster, the family retriever, trotted in on Ty's heels and rubbed up against Clara's leg to say hello with a wag of his tail.

"Go lie down, Buster," Clara said firmly. "Last thing I need is you in my biscuit dough."

The dog obediently found his bed in the corner and curled up on it.

Ty looked around, saw Virgil sleeping, and an indulgent smile curved his lips. She looked down to cover her surprise. The smile changed his face completely, softening his jaw and cheekbones, erasing years off his face and making it appear almost boyish.

Clara slid the pan into the oven, determined to finally put things on an even keel. "Good morning, Tyson." She deliberately kept her voice pleasant and impersonal.

He tilted his head, studying her as she straightened, brushing off her hands. "Ty, remember? Unless I'm in trouble, it's Ty." The smile changed, his lips curving in a devilish grin. "Does calling me Tyson mean you're still mad?"

In trouble? He *was* trouble. It would have been easier if he hadn't smiled, she realized. His smile was the one thing she couldn't get out of her head. At the wedding it had been warm, intimate and slightly lopsided as though he was sharing a joke. The warmth of it had extended to his eyes, the brown-as-molasses depths of them with sun-drenched crinkles in the corners.

She avoided his gaze and set the timer on the oven instead. He thought she was mad? Embarrassed, yes. Awkward—definitely. Angry? Well, maybe a little. He shouldn't have rubbed his lips over her temple like that. It was presumptuous. It was...

Glorious. It had made her feel feminine and alive. Lordy, but he was a distraction! She wished he'd get out of the kitchen and back to the barns so she could focus better.

"Miss Ferguson?"

She was surprised that he persisted in addressing her so formally—to the rest of the family she was just Clara. His sober tone turned her head and she bit down on her lip at the sight of him, his weight on one hip, all well-worn jeans and a long-sleeved shirt, the grin no longer in sight. He wore a baseball cap. The curved peak made him seem—for the second time in as many minutes—ridiculously young. She had to stop noticing and simply do her job. It was the most important thing right now, her ticket to a new life. She was saving as much as she could so she could afford her own place. And Ty Diamond wasn't going to screw that up for her.

"Did you want to ask me something?"

He hesitated so long that Clara fought the urge to squirm. The timer on the oven ticked down painfully slowly. Virgil, asleep in his favorite chair in the living room, let out a random snore. It broke the silence, and alleviated a bit of the tension. Clara let out a soft laugh as Virgil snored again and shifted in his chair.

"Your father always falls asleep during his crossword," she said quietly. She wasn't quite sure what to call Virgil in reference to Ty. He was Ty's adopted dad but also his uncle by blood. And the tension between the two sometimes made her wonder if they even acknowledged each other as relatives at all.

"He gets tired easily, doesn't he?"

She nodded. "The stroke took a lot out of him. He's made wonderful progress, though. He did great in his physio this morning. Even if it did take a lot of prodding and a fair amount of sass."

"From you or from him?" Ty's eyes seemed to twinkle at her.

"From him, of course. He's been irritable lately." She met his gaze with a look that told him she knew the source of Virgil's displeasure.

"That's probably my fault," Ty admitted. "He's changed more than I expected. Sam warned me. About a lot of things."

His gaze was steady on her again and the ridiculous fluttering she'd felt at the wedding came dancing back. What had Sam warned him about? That Virgil was more stubborn than ever? That things weren't exactly calm and peaceful around Diamondback Ranch? Or had he warned Ty of something else—about *someone* else? A sudden thought struck. Had Ty asked her to dance because he'd been put up to it?

Each time she thought of that night she regretted it more.

"I'm just his nurse," Clara replied, turning away and taking the rolling pin and empty biscuit bowl to the sink.

"I didn't realize nurse duties included baking." He stepped forward and snuck a small bit of raw biscuit dough from the countertop, popping it in his mouth.

Clara felt a sharp and sudden pain in her heart, watching him sneak the scrap of dough. How many times had she and her brother done that as kids? Bread dough, cookie dough, it hadn't mattered. Their mother would scold but never yell, saying that she hoped they had children someday who did the same thing and drove them crazy. The memory sent a bitter pang through Clara's heart. Life had been so uncomplicated then.

Clara missed her family terribly. She'd followed Jackson to Alberta when he'd claimed he'd make his money in the oil patch and set them up for life. She'd been blind and stupid to leave all the good things behind to chase empty promises. But it was too late to go back home now. How could she possibly explain the changes over the years that had passed? No, the gulf was too wide. Saskatchewan was only a province away but it might as well have been a continent.

"I like to cook, and it gives Molly more of a chance to get out now and again," Clara explained. Besides, if she wasn't here at Diamondback, she was home at Butterfly House, and lately she'd felt more and more dissatisfied with that arrangement. She wanted her own place. Her own space and her own things. She wanted to buy her own groceries and eat on her own schedule and not worry about a set chore list.

"Did you make the pumpkin bread yesterday?"

She wiped her hands on a dishtowel.

"I did, yes."

"It was very good."

It felt so stilted and practiced, Clara realized. She lifted her chin. At least Ty was making an effort for the first time since the wedding. Maybe they just needed to clear the air and find some common ground. He'd never answered her first question so she repeated it.

"Is there something you wanted, Ty?"

The tiny smile threatened to mar the perfection of his

lips. She'd called him Ty deliberately and according to his wishes. Maybe if they could move past the Tyson and Miss Ferguson bit it would be more comfortable.

"Hang on. I'll be right back."

He disappeared up the stairs. Clara ran water into the sink, preparing to wash up her dishes. In seconds he was back, holding her shawl in his hands.

"You dropped this the other night," he said quietly. "I thought you might want it back."

She'd wondered where she'd misplaced it, but was so embarrassed about her quick exit that she hadn't had the courage to ask Molly if it had been found. She dried her hands on a dishtowel and took it from him, careful not to touch his hands. "Thank you. I wondered where it went."

Silence filled the kitchen once more, a quiet of the awkward variety. When she couldn't stand it any longer, she put her dishcloth back in the water and turned to face him. "Was there something else?"

"I don't quite know how to say it," he admitted, then reached up and took off his ball cap. His sable hair was slightly flattened and the band of the cap created a ring around his head.

"Just spit it out," she suggested, her tummy doing weird and wonderful things. Tyson Diamond exuded a carelessness that practically shouted *bad boy*. But most bad boys she'd known growing up had been overconfident and pushy. Not Ty. He was just…there. With his intense eyes and slow swagger. It wasn't much wonder the women flocked to him. Ty didn't have to do anything more than breathe. And here she was, hanging on his every word.

And she knew what it was like to be pressed up against his lean body.

And why on earth was she thinking such a thing?

He frowned, jamming his hands into his pockets. "I'm sorry for the other night. I upset you and I didn't mean to."

Her lips dropped open. Ty was apologizing? He thought she was mad at him—and she was, she supposed, but only a little bit. She'd been the one to ask him to dance. She'd been the one who'd quite unexpectedly melted in his arms. Yes, he'd gotten quite close and then he'd suggested they get out of there, but he hadn't truly done anything so very wrong.

She couldn't have asked for someone to be gentler with her as they'd danced. He'd tipped up her chin and put himself into her hands, letting her take the lead. It wasn't his suggestion that had upset her. It was the fact that she'd wanted to take him up on that offer so badly she'd frightened herself. For a brief, heady moment she'd considered taking his hand and letting him lead her away.

And then she'd come to her senses. She wasn't anywhere near ready to let something like that happen. And then there was the fact that for a few precious minutes she'd forgotten all about her plans and goals and let herself weaken. Oh, she hadn't been mad at Ty. She'd been furious with *herself.*

"You don't need to apologize. Let's just forget the whole thing." She made a show of picking up a set of oven mitts, wishing the oven timer would ding so she could be doing something, anything, rather than feel pinned beneath Ty's dark gaze. She chanced a look up and saw that his eyes had warmed.

"Did you think I was angry?" she asked bravely, suddenly wanting to know. She thought perhaps she'd prefer that to him thinking she was silly and weak.

He opened his lips to answer when the oven timer dinged—just when she wanted to hear his answer.

With a frown of consternation she opened the oven door

and slid out the pan of golden-brown biscuits. She put the pan on top of the stove.

"I wondered," he replied, "because you ran. I wondered if it was because of…you know, your past. I didn't think about that when I…well…it wasn't really a kiss, was it?"

She kept her back to him, closing her eyes. It was a small town and the Butterfly House project was a big deal around here. It was no secret that she came from an abusive background. Of course she was damaged goods.

"I'm not angry. It was just wedding fever or something. I blew what happened out of proportion. You have been perfectly polite and kind to me since you came home."

"Then why won't you look at me right now?"

Her gaze darted up to look into his face. He was too serious. When he looked at her that way it was twice as bad as when he flirted with his saucy grin. "Why did you do it?" she whispered. She didn't need to elaborate for them both to know what "it" was.

"Why did you ask, after you made it clear you didn't want to dance?"

She grabbed a dishcloth and began wiping off the counter. "I thought maybe I'd hurt your feelings."

He laughed, a sharp sound of disbelief as he leaned against the island. "Hurt my feelings? Clara, I think I'm made of tougher stuff than that."

She was getting annoyed now at being put on the spot. "Well then I'm sorry I did it. You can take your unhurt feelings and quit cluttering up my kitchen!"

But it wasn't her kitchen, and they were both aware of it. Silence settled over them, bringing that same, damnable feeling of intimacy she could never escape when he was around.

"You felt good in my arms," he said quietly. "And that's not a line. It's the only reason I have for losing my head.

It's not the sort of situation I normally find myself in. It was innocent, I swear. But I forgot what it's like here in Cadence Creek. It probably opened you up to speculation and for that I'm sorry. It won't happen again."

His explanation—his apology—touched her, though she would rather not let it show. It was better for everyone if they really did forget that stupid dance had ever happened.

"Yes, I think that's best." Thank goodness he was being sensible about it all. "I'm pretty focused on what I want, Tyson. I'm not interested in distractions. And right now my job is to help your father get well."

"I'll stay out of your way," he replied.

He'd been absent during the long weeks when his father was sick. He hadn't come home even when they'd asked him to. But he was here now, and she didn't like the idea that she might be standing in the way of him settling in. Of mending fences. Virgil had a habit of talking to himself and Clara had heard snatches of mutterings and grumblings. Virgil was not happy with his younger son. It wasn't good for him to be stressed. He and Ty needed to sort things out.

"You need to be with your father. I know you stayed away a long time, Tyson. He needs you. As long as we're clear, there's no need to avoid each other, right?"

She bent to get a cooling rack out of the cupboard and started piling the biscuits on the top.

Tyson's gaze caught on the golden-brown biscuits as the warm scent filled the air. She brushed her hands on her apron and stood back. Good God, she was pretty. The dark ringlets from the wedding were gone but now her hair fell in gentle waves to her shoulders. And her eyes... They were the same blue as a September sky over the golden prairie. Her plain apron covered the soft curves of her hips. He was shocked to realize he wanted to put his hands on them and pull her close to see if her lips tasted as sweet as they looked.

But she was sweet, and off-limits. Never mind that he had no idea how to really talk to her. The past ten minutes had been torturous, second-guessing his words and meaning. All his normal self-assurance evaporated when faced with a woman like Clara Ferguson.

He pushed the thoughts aside and nodded at the rack of biscuits. "Mind if I try one?"

"Sure. Here." She gave him a paper napkin and one of the round golden discs. He went to the cupboard and found the carton of molasses. Moments later he'd split the biscuit open and slathered it with butter and the sticky spread.

It was like biting into a buttery cloud. Better than his mother's, if that were possible. In four bites it was gone. Wordlessly she held out another.

"These are delicious, Clara."

"My mother's recipe."

He chewed and swallowed. He had a fair amount of experience dealing with whispers and gossip, and most of the time it ran off him like water off a duck's back. He didn't give a good damn about what Cadence Creek thought. But he found he cared what *she* thought. In some ways she was right. He did need more time with Virgil. He just had no idea how to go about it without starting an argument.

"The reason I stayed away, well, it's complicated."

She nodded. "It usually is. Molly said you didn't even come for his seventieth birthday a few years back. They had a big party I guess. But you wouldn't come."

"I couldn't come," he said.

"Couldn't or wouldn't?"

He wanted her to know why, but telling her could be a huge mistake. He'd had a good reason, but spending a few nights in lockup sounded bad no matter how he spun it. With her history he just couldn't bring himself to say it.

"Do you think it was the right thing for me to come home now?" he asked. He shifted his gaze to look at Virgil, still sleeping in his chair. Virgil had aged so much. He was smaller now than Ty ever remembered, and looked so vulnerable. Ty hated that. Hated that he might have been part of the cause of his father aging, too, by leaving Virgil more of the ranch to handle than he should have.

"Yes," Clara said firmly. "Yes, I do. For your brother, who needed you, and for your mom. Molly missed you and talked about you often. She felt terrible about the rift between you and your dad. And for Virgil, too, of course."

"He criticizes everything I do. He'd be happier if I'd stayed on the circuit and never come home." Even as he said it, he heard how childish it sounded, and he wasn't sure it was true. Virgil had always insisted that it was Ty's place to be at Diamondback pulling his weight. But it was always Virgil's way or no way at all. Ty had chafed against all that authority.

Clara put down the mug she was holding and peered up into Tyson's face. He didn't like that she seemed to see what he took great care to keep hidden. He'd excelled at his chosen path and had the trophies and accolades to prove it. But inside was a boy who always felt second-best.

"You need to patch things up," she reiterated. "What are you waiting for?"

Virgil shifted in his chair and let out a moan as he woke from his nap. What was Ty waiting for? He was excited about his new idea but he knew Virgil would think it was stupid. He wanted to say he was sorry but knew he'd just be told he was being weak.

If he was waiting for unconditional love, he'd be waiting a long time, and it was too hard to take the first step.

Ty reached for his hat, putting it back on his head. "I'd better get back to work."

Clara sighed as the door closed behind him and he passed by the kitchen window, his long legs eating up the ground. "I think the person who needed you to come home the most was you, Ty," she murmured at his retreating back. And she had no idea how to help either one of them meet in the middle.

CHAPTER THREE

As much as Clara loved her job at Diamondback, Virgil's care was not enough for the full-time hours she was paid. Sometimes she felt like a glorified housekeeper. Not that it was a problem, but one of these days Molly was going to let her go and she'd have to find a new job. She would probably have to leave Cadence Creek; her stay at Butterfly House was only temporary until she could get on her feet. She'd been squirreling away money, but it cost a lot for an apartment and all the furniture she'd need.

She needed this job for as long as it held out and she was going to wring every drop out of the opportunity.

But for now she was sitting in one of the spare rooms, needle and thimble in hand, making tiny, even stitches in Molly's latest quilt.

She enjoyed doing things with her hands. As a girl she'd learned to cross-stitch and knit; she and her mother had spent evenings in front of the television working on little projects. It had been her mom's way of unwinding after working all day in an office, and it had been Clara's way of spending time with her mom.

She'd spent a lot of time thinking about her mom lately. She'd learned so much from her mother, but the lesson that Clara carried now was how she had always insisted that a woman needed a way to support herself. No matter what, Wendy Ferguson had put in a good day's work and still had time for her kids. As Clara fed the needle through the fabric, she missed her mother something terrible. She talked to Ty about mending fences, so maybe once she was settled she'd reach out to Wendy, too. Maybe they could be a part of each other's lives again.

But for now Molly sat across from Clara, her own needle flashing in and out as she made stitches on the patterned lines of fabric.

"It's almost ready to roll," Molly remarked, tying off her thread and moving to cut a new piece.

The quilt was tied onto old-fashioned wood frames with metal brackets holding the corners. Once they'd quilted as far as they could reach comfortably, the frame would be rolled in and clamped tight. When it was all done Molly would bind the perimeter. But that was weeks away yet, especially since they only sneaked the occasional hour to work on it.

"It's beautiful," Clara replied. "The burgundy-and-green pattern is stunning against the cream."

They stitched for a few more moments, but Clara got the sense that Molly wanted to say something. She shifted in her chair and there was a tension around them that usually didn't exist. Clara's fingers tightened on the needle. Did Molly have a concern about Virgil's care? Or was it something else? Molly, along with the rest of Cadence Creek, had surely seen Clara run from Ty at the wedding. She'd probably seen how close they'd danced, too. And she would be foolish to think the older woman hadn't noticed the strain around the house since his arrival. There was no question that despite breaking the ice, Clara and Ty still tiptoed around each other.

"Is something wrong, Molly?"

Molly put down her needle and sighed. "I suppose so, Clara. I find myself feeling a little bit selfish these days."

Molly? Selfish? Impossible. Clara tied off her thread and snipped it with the scissors. "I don't think you know how to be selfish, Molly." She smiled, but inside she was feeling a bit uneasy.

"No, I am," she admitted. "I have gotten used to having you here. I *like* having you here. And I have taken terrible advantage of you."

Clara's head swam with confusion. Advantage? She had so much to thank Molly for. If anything, Clara felt like she was taking advantage of the Diamonds' generosity. "You gave me a job when I needed one, Molly. You made me feel welcome from the moment I arrived."

"Virgil's care is not a full-time job, Clara, and I feel I've kept you here when you might have found another better position somewhere else. And I've kept you for my own selfish reasons that have nothing to do with medical care."

A cold line of dread snuck down Clara's spine. Was this Molly's gentle way of letting her go? She could look for something else, but it would mean she'd be even longer getting into her own place. She swallowed against the growing lump in her throat. It wasn't just the money either. She'd come to care for Molly and Virgil very much. She already knew it was going to be difficult to say goodbye when the time came.

Molly sighed and began stitching again. "I never had a daughter around, you see. Never had someone to cook with or talk to or sit and quilt with. It was all boys all the time, and I've enjoyed having you here so much. But you're a nurse, Clara, not a hired companion. I just want you to know that if you were to find another position it's okay. I'd miss you, but I'd understand."

Clara swallowed again as relief made her wilt on the inside. "You're not letting me go, then?"

Molly lifted startled eyes to Clara's. "Heavens, no! Was that what you thought?"

Clara's cheeks heated. "I thought you were letting me down easy."

"Oh, goodness." Molly's eyes softened with compassion. "We all adore you. But this is about you, not us."

All adore her? She doubted it. Obviously Molly hadn't included Ty in that equation. Since their talk things had been a bit easier, but it was a long way from being totally comfortable, and adoration was a joke.

"I'll stay as long as you feel Virgil needs my help," she replied carefully. "Honestly, Molly, sometimes I feel guilty taking a paycheck." She offered a smile.

"How much longer are you staying at Butterfly House, then?" Molly didn't look up but her stitches seemed to slow.

"I've been saving up for my own place," Clara explained. "The program is great, but if I can find an apartment, that frees up my spot for someone else who needs it more."

Molly's voice remained conversational as she stitched along a dark green leaf. "This job could easily include room and board."

Clara's heart leapt. Oh, that was generous and so very *Molly.* And a few weeks ago she might have accepted—especially with Angela and Sam getting married and moving into their new house soon. But now there was Ty. It shouldn't matter that he lived here now, too, but somehow it did.

"Oh, Molly, that's so kind of you to offer, but I can't do that. You've been far too good to me already."

Molly's soft eyes met hers. "You're already like one of

the family. It doesn't make sense for you to have to scrimp and save when there is plenty of room here."

But there was every reason, and not just because of Ty. "I wouldn't hurt your feelings for the world, so I hope when I say that this is something I need to do on my own—on my own two feet—you understand. I know you're offering from your heart, and that means so much." Her throat tightened with emotion. "But I can't stay here. I need my own place, my own space. And even though I know you don't mean it that way, I would feel a bit like a charity case."

"Of course I understand." Molly smiled. "I told you I was being selfish. And I'll confess, I'm a bit relieved that you're not going anywhere for a while. You've made all our lives easier."

Except Ty's, Clara thought dryly. She put her needle to work again. Every time he came into a room where she was, he got this weird look on his face before masking it away.

And despite her assertions that she needed independence, she knew darn well she'd be tempted to take up the offer if it didn't mean being faced with Ty twenty-four-seven. Morning, noon and night. Running into each other in the hallways. Sleeping down the hall from each other...

That thought made something delicious hum inside her and *that* was how she knew it was trouble. Trouble she wouldn't touch with a ten-foot pole.

They worked together until they'd each finished the side they were stitching. Molly took a few moments to check on Virgil, who was watching television, and came back with Ty in tow.

"Look who I found hovering around the doughnut jar. Just the help we need to roll the quilt."

Ty's eyes met hers and their gazes caught for one

breathless moment. Goodness, she didn't know why he
had the power to make her feel all fizzy and flustered. He
looked so *ordinary,* after all, dressed in plain jeans and a
plaid work shirt, with his hair still slightly messy. One of
Ty's eyebrows rose as he spoke to Molly but kept his gaze
locked on Clara. "I haven't rolled a quilt since…"

"Since you were a teenager and still at home, and you
and Sam did the rolling while I put on the clamps," Molly
finished.

Ty looked down on the top of Molly's head. Clara hid
a smile. Ty was what, close to thirty? It had to be con-
stricting for a grown man to be back in his childhood bed
again after years of living on his own.

"I haven't forgotten how," he replied, going to one end
of the quilt. "Mom, you and I can roll and Clara can do
the clamps."

Molly braced her hip against one of the frame pieces
and held everything taut while Clara removed the clamps.
Then together Molly and Tyson pulled the fabric tight and
rolled it under—once, twice, three times.

"Okay, Clara. Put the clamps back on."

She did Molly's corner first because it was harder for
the older woman to hold the frame tight and steady. Once
that was done she went to Ty's side. But the room was
small and she had to brush by him to get the right angle.
Their bodies touched—absolutely innocently—but she
noticed all the same. She could see the bulge of Ty's arm
muscles through his shirt as he held the frame taut. She
put the clamp over the intersection of frame pieces but it
slipped out of her hands and clattered to the floor.

Rattled, she bent and retrieved the clamp and hurried
to tighten it to the frame.

But when they finished they still had to do the other
side. And no one was talking. She had to stop clamming

up every time he entered a room. Maybe she *should* be looking for a job somewhere else. But then she thought of Molly's kind face and Virgil's rusty laugh and she knew she had to stay. She also knew that refusing the offer of room and board was for the best. She couldn't even roll a quilt with Ty without getting flustered. Living under the same roof would be torture. She wasn't stupid. She had all the signs of being hopelessly attracted to him and yet she shied away from the simplest of touches. Touches that she really didn't want, seeing as touches usually led to other things called complications.

This time she shoved the clamp over the boards and tightened it with sure hands.

"Thanks, you two," Molly said, brushing her hands and looking oblivious to the undercurrents running between Ty and Clara. Perhaps Clara was imagining them. Ty adjusted the stand beneath their corner of the frame and straightened, squaring his shoulders.

"You're welcome. I should get back now." He shuffled past the quilt towards the door. "Lots to do before quitting time."

Ty couldn't get out of the room fast enough, Clara thought. She had to stop letting him affect her like this.

When Ty left, she let out a breath. Why couldn't things stay the way they'd been two, even three weeks ago? Before Ty came back? She had been comfortable coming to work, enjoyed feeling as if she belonged here. Now she was restless, on edge. Feeling that everything was going to change. She'd had enough change to last a lifetime— she didn't need any more.

She knew the answer, she thought, as she stuck her needle into the spool of thread and left it on top of the quilt. Nothing was the same since Ty came because she'd asked him to dance. Because she'd been in his arms and had felt his strong jaw against her temple, his wide hand along the small of her back.

And those few minutes had unlocked something inside her—an old longing, a need for something more. Something she hadn't imagined she'd ever want again. A something more that terrified her to the soles of her shoes. For a physical relationship would only be temporary, and an emotional one would make her far too vulnerable.

Gray clouds had rolled in over the prairie sky hours earlier and the north wind hadn't let up. October was early in the fall for snow, but Ty knew stranger things had happened. A few errant flakes wouldn't surprise him in the least. He shrugged into his jacket, turning up the collar before leaving the barn. He looked up at the house. The lights in the kitchen glowed warmly, but all Ty felt was dread.

His mother was overly cheerful to the point of annoyance right now. He knew she was trying to keep the peace—like today, when she'd pressed him into helping with the quilt. She wanted things to go back to the way they were when he'd been a boy, but that was impossible. Things had been said that couldn't be taken back. He was a grown man. And then there was Clara, all big eyes and as jumpy as a spring frog. She couldn't even get within a foot of him without getting flustered. He'd thought that apologizing to her might ease her discomfort, but today she'd dropped the clamp and hadn't looked at him again before he'd gotten the hell out of there.

And then there was Virgil. All his dad did was scowl. It bugged Ty that Virgil had apparently butted heads with Sam all summer but now it seemed Sam could do no wrong. Of course now Ty was home and he supposed Sam looked like angel in comparison. No matter how he tried to smooth things over, it felt as though all he was doing was stirring up a hornet's nest. One of these days someone was going to get stung.

He slid the barn door shut and latched it. The hell of it all was he loved his dad. Seeking approval that never came had driven him crazy; it had been easier to leave and do his own thing than stay and argue indefinitely, or feel that he could never live up to expectations.

But he was getting older. And so was Virgil. When Sam had called, Ty knew it was time to go home. He thought maybe they'd all mellowed over the past few years. That it would be different.

Mellowed, hah. Ty had walked in the door, Virgil had taken one look and muttered "Humph" before turning away.

It had been a deliberate slap. Ty wished he were a stronger man. That it didn't matter. But it did. Virgil was the only father he'd ever known. He hadn't wanted to adopt Ty, but he had anyway. Ty had spent years trying to prove to Virgil that it hadn't been a mistake. That he was worthy of the Diamond name.

How sad did that make him? He imagined what Virgil would say if he came out and admitted such a thing. He'd tell Ty he was weak. That a man only had to prove something to himself.

An odd whirring sound caught his ear and he paused. There it was again—like a car trying to turn over. He looked towards the garage and saw the bumper of Clara's car, mostly hidden by the farm 4x4.

He sighed, knowing dinner waited inside, knowing she probably didn't want his help but also knowing he couldn't just leave her there. She was going to flood the thing if she kept it up. He made his way over, shoving his hands in his pockets against the raw air. She was behind the wheel, turning the key and looking more than a little frazzled. The late-model car looked as if it was being held together with baler twine and bubble gum. The click-and-whir sounded again as Ty knocked on the window.

She rolled it down—the car was so old it still had manual windows. "My car won't start. I think my battery is dead."

"I'll give you a boost. How old is your battery?"

"Um, I don't know. I bought the car secondhand."

Clearly. It was a "Point A to Point B" car, and even that was being generous. "Don't worry, I'll have you home in no time."

He grabbed the keys from his pocket and went into the garage, starting his car rather than using the farm truck. The engine roared to life, the 454 block engine growling like a leashed lion. The seat was molded perfectly to the shape of his backside. The fact that the classic car felt more like home than the house he grew up in wasn't lost on him.

He backed out and parked it in position ahead of her car. He popped the hood and raised it up, anchoring it in place before doing likewise to her car and then connecting the battery cables. "Try it now," he said, and she turned the key.

The engine sputtered and started and he watched as a big smile filled her face. She looked great when she smiled, which wasn't that often, he noticed. She went through the motions, and she gave pleasant little polite smiles, but not a real, genuine grin like this. She looked like a whole other person when she relaxed. Her whole face lit up—just the way it had on the night of the wedding. It made her eyes shine and her skin glow. At first glance Ty had thought her rather unremarkable. But when she let down her guard, he realized she was quite pretty but in a softer, plainer way than he was used to. Her smile slid away as if she'd just realized she was doing it and was autocorrecting.

He unhooked the cables and backed the car away. When he hopped out, Clara was waiting beside her door, the engine still running. "Thanks, Ty. I guess I'll have to see about a new battery."

"If it doesn't start in the morning, call and I'll come get you."

She drew back a little and he wondered if her assertion the other day that she wasn't afraid was the truth or a convenient lie.

"I should be able to get a battery here in town, right?"

"At Pritchett's Auto."

"I'd better get going. You haven't even had your supper yet. Thanks again."

"You bet."

He had his hand on his car-door handle when her voice called out again. "Ty?"

He turned back. At least she was calling him Ty. She must not be mad anymore.

"Um, shouldn't the voltage thingy go up?"

Yes, he thought, it should. He went back to her car, stuck his head in and checked her dashboard. The car had been running a few minutes now and should be holding a better charge. He frowned and slid behind the wheel, turning off the key. After a few seconds he tried to start it again—dead.

"I don't think it's your battery."

A quick look at the contacts showed little corrosion. "It might be your alternator. Hang on a minute." He went into the garage and came out with a test meter. "I think it's dead, Clara."

"How much will it cost to fix?" She worried her lower lip with her teeth. Ty watched as the supple pink flesh was released, regaining its full, delicious shape. Right. The last thing he needed to focus on was Clara's lips. She was his dad's nurse, for Pete's sake. And she was carrying around a lot of baggage. He had to nip those sorts of thoughts in the bud right now. She couldn't even stand being in the same room with him.

"A couple hundred for the parts, maybe a bit less if you buy a rebuilt one instead of new. And I can put it in for you and save you the labor."

"Oh."

He could almost see the calculator running in her brain. "If it's too much, I can pay for it and you can pay me back a little at a time."

"No!" She stood up straighter. "It's not that. I'm just trying to save up for my own place and stuff. I can dip into my savings."

So she had her own bit of pride, he thought, pleased even though his offer had been genuine. "I thought you were staying at Butterfly House."

"It's temporary," she replied, putting her hands in her coat pockets. "The program is just to get women on their feet as they start over, you know?"

"And you're ready for that?"

She nodded. "I'm ready to be in charge of my own life. But for right now that means putting aside what I can each week so I can come up with first and last month's rent. That sort of thing."

She was stronger than she appeared, Ty thought. At times she seemed unbearably shy and quite jumpy. Her whole body had tensed when their bodies had brushed today. She rarely met his gaze, too. But when she did, it was usually with a determination he admired. Clara Ferguson was no pushover. He liked that.

"Well, you're not going anywhere in that car tonight," he said. "Grab your purse and I'll drive you home."

She hesitated and he knew that despite her words to the contrary, being alone with him made her uneasy.

"You could always call a cab. Or walk." He said the words with a smile. They both knew there was no cab in Cadence Creek and that Diamondback was a good five miles from Butterfly House.

"Funny," she answered dryly, putting her hand on the car-door handle.

The interior of the car was small and felt confined with her in it beside him. Country music played on the radio, filling the space with welcome sound. Clara said nothing, just stared out the window at the brown fields as he put the car in gear and it rumbled down the driveway.

"Your car is…old." She finally broke the awkward silence.

He tried a smile. "I prefer classic."

"What is it?"

"A 1970 Chevelle SS. I bought it for cheap in Edmonton a few years back and restored it."

"You did?"

"Yeah. I worked on it over the winters."

"You're a pretty handy guy to have around. Any other talents up your sleeve?"

He shrugged. "A few, maybe. I like working with my hands. And I got used to doing things for myself."

Silence fell in the car as he turned onto the main road. Several seconds ticked by, feeling interminably long as she stared out the window at the barren fields.

"How's Dad tonight?" he asked, anything to break the awkward quiet. He was starting to wonder if anything would ever be natural between them. If he'd ever stop second-guessing what he said around her, afraid of saying the wrong thing.

"Good. Tired. I think he's getting this cold that's been going around, and I want to make sure it doesn't go to his chest. He's got an appointment on Friday so we'll see how it goes. He ate his supper in his room, though. I've been trying to get him to eat in the kitchen with Molly more often."

"He doesn't do anything he doesn't want to," Ty replied, knowing exactly how tough the man could be when he made up his mind. An immovable brick wall.

"Oh, he's not as tough as you might think. You just have to know how to get around him." She smiled but Ty didn't share in it. After thirty years, he should know how to get around Virgil. But he didn't.

"Maybe you can tell me your secrets sometime," he answered, perhaps a little sharply. He looked over at Clara and let out a breath. "Sorry. I'm a little touchy where my dad is concerned."

She laughed. "Touchy? I hadn't noticed."

Oh, so she had a sense of sarcasm in there after all. He focused on the road but relaxed. "So what'd I miss at dinner tonight?"

"Chicken pot pie."

It sounded like heaven. Creamy chicken and vegetables, sopping up the gravy with fresh bread. His stomach nearly growled just thinking about it. "I'm sorry I missed it."

"You wouldn't if you stopped avoiding the house."

"It's that obvious?"

She nodded. "Yes. I just haven't figured out if you're avoiding your father or avoiding me."

His fingers tightened on the wheel. "Does it matter? It's easier for everyone if I just keep my distance, isn't it?"

They pulled into the Butterfly House yard. He put the car into park but left it running.

She turned in her seat and looked at him. "I don't want to keep you from spending time with your father. He needs that, Ty."

"I don't want to stress him out."

"You could try talking to him."

"Which always ends in an argument."

She huffed. "Good Lord, the both of you are stubborn. If you want to keep things the way they are, then fine. But your father is not going to be here forever, Ty. He might be recovering from his stroke but he is seventy-three years old. You might want to try a little harder."

His fingers tightened on the wheel as the words to explain sat on his tongue. "I'll get the part for your car tomorrow and give you the receipt. Good night, Clara."

Her face flattened. "Good night, Ty. Thank you for the drive."

She got out and slammed the door.

He put his head on the steering wheel for a few seconds as she made her way up the drive to the Butterfly House door.

"Dammit," he muttered, shut off the ignition and got out. "Clara, wait."

She paused by the door.

"I don't know how to talk to him," he said. It felt good to say it at last. And a bit scary.

Clara was standing with the key to the house in her hand. She tucked it back into her purse, turned her back on the house and met his gaze.

"Buy me a piece of pie," she said, straightening her shoulders.

CHAPTER FOUR

THE WAGON WHEEL DINER was the only place to eat in Cadence Creek except the sandwich counter at the gas station.

Clara walked in with Ty and felt a dozen sets of eyes on them. She tried to ignore them. This was not a date. People would always speculate, wouldn't they? And while being in a restaurant with Ty felt weird, it was nothing compared to being alone with him. This was much safer. Another step in her progress, right? Besides, this was about Virgil. The tension between Virgil and Ty was taking its toll. It wasn't good for him to be so stressed. If she could help the two of them meet in the middle it would be so much better for everyone at Diamondback.

Ty led her to a table in a back corner and, to her surprise, held out her chair as she sat down.

Not the first time he'd behaved gallantly. She suspected there might be a gem inside Ty Diamond after all—if he could get rid of the huge chip on his shoulder. Not that it mattered to her. She was only here to help Virgil. The older man had his share of grumpiness but she'd grown fond of him. He had a way of looking up at her with his eyes snapping that made her smile.

Ty had the same look, whether he knew it or not.

"Some things never change," Ty said, pushing aside a menu and relaxing against the wooden chair back. "Martha Bullock's been cooking here for over twenty years and, thank God, has no desire to retire."

"You used to come here," Clara said.

"Since I was a kid. Some kids saved nickels and dimes for candy at the store. I saved it for a piece of Martha's lemon meringue pie."

A waitress approached and took out a small notepad. "Well. Tyson Diamond. Ain't you a sight."

She had to be fifty if she was a day, but her lashes fluttered all the same. Clara rolled her eyes. She'd been absolutely right. All Tyson had to do was breathe and the women fell over themselves. This one was old enough to be his mother!

"Judy. How's George?"

"Gonna take me on a second honeymoon for our twenty-fifth, he says. Told me to pack a bathing suit for Mexico. Can you believe that?"

"You deserve it," Ty said with a wink. "Twenty-five years. Somethin' to celebrate for sure. Have you met Dad's nurse, Clara?"

Judy gave a wide smile. "Virgil still as ornery as ever?"

Clara grinned back. "He's a pussycat."

Judy laughed and Ty angled an appraising look at Clara. "You can see why Mom calls her a miracle worker, eh, Judy?"

Clara felt a glow start deep inside. He'd deliberately made it clear she was here as his father's nurse. Not that it would stop small-town gossip. She'd known that when she suggested it. But he was trying. He understood. And that meant something.

"I missed dinner," she heard him say. "I'd kill for one of Martha's hot turkey sandwiches and a slice of lemon pie."

"You got it. Clara?"

"Coconut cream if you've got it. And a cup of tea, please."

"Coming right up."

With a pat on Ty's shoulder she was gone, leaving them alone with the sound of the jukebox filling up the silence left in her wake.

"All the weeks I've been here, I haven't come into the diner," she said to Ty. An old George Jones tune twanged in the background. "That's a real jukebox, isn't it?"

He grinned. "Some things never change." His smile slipped a bit. "Sometimes that's good. Sometimes not so much."

She folded her hands in her lap. "You're talking about your father." It was so much easier talking to Ty when it was about Virgil, not herself. It almost felt ordinary. It had been years since her life had felt ordinary. It was spectacularly odd and comforting at the same time.

"We never see eye to eye. And the harder I try, the more we argue. That's why I left in the first place. We were going to say something that we couldn't fix, you know? I couldn't do it anymore."

"So you became a rodeo star."

There was that sexy grin again. "It didn't start out that way. I left in rebellion and I went to work at a place in Caroline. I was seventeen and feeling indestructible. A few broken bones, the odd scar, but I was good at it. It was a rush and there were..." He paused, as if measuring his words. "Benefits," he finished, but his dark eyes were sparkling devilishly at her.

"So why come home now?"

He shrugged. "Because I can't ride bulls forever. Because Sam asked me to."

"To make amends?" she asked carefully.

"I don't know if that's possible."

Judy came back with Ty's meal and Clara's pie and tea. Clara dipped the tea bag in the cup, bobbing it up and down a few times before squeezing it along the side with her spoon.

"Of course it's possible," she said quietly. "You just have to be willing to try."

She added a touch of milk to her tea and took a sip. Ty dipped a French fry in gravy, swirling it around his plate thoughtfully. "I don't know what he wants from me. Growing up I never felt like anything I did was good enough. There was so much pressure."

"From him or from yourself?"

His hand stopped moving and he stared at her. "What do you mean?"

She shrugged, picked up her fork and made an effort to cut into her pie. "I just wondered if you were always aware of the difference between you and Sam and if you felt like you were second-best."

He picked up his fork and stabbed the sandwich. "That's blunt." He sawed off a corner of the gravy-soaked bread. "You know, most of the time you have this whole sweet vibe going on, but then you really know how to put a guy in his place."

"Thank you." She couldn't help the smile that curved her lips.

"Thank you?" He popped the forkful of food in his mouth and raised his eyebrows at her.

"A few months ago I wouldn't even have been sitting here across from you, let alone speaking honestly. I know all about low self-esteem, Ty. I struggle with it daily. So telling me I have an assertive streak is a huge compliment."

"I guess you're really not afraid of me, then."

"I wouldn't go that far. It would depend on how you defined *afraid.*"

The funny swirling silence enveloped them once more and Clara's stomach turned to butterflies. The first time they'd truly spoken there'd been attraction. Since then it had been awkward and stilted. But this—this was a whole other set of nerves. And it was as delicious as the custardy pie filling sitting on her tongue.

They knew each other a little better now, and the familiarity was starting to breed comfort.

"I'm sorry for what happened to you," he replied, putting down his fork. "I might not see eye to eye with my dad, but I think we can agree that a man should never hit a woman. I hope you know you're safe with me."

Clara studied his face, debating whether or not she should reveal any bits of her story. It was so intensely private. So painful. And yet by keeping it inside like a dirty secret, she was giving it power, wasn't she?

"Before I met Jackson, I never thought I'd be one of *those* women. I'd be smarter. I'd be stronger. And then there I was, believing all the things he said. Thinking it was my fault. Too afraid to leave, trying to do the right things so it wouldn't happen again. Making excuses—for him and for myself. That person is not who I am. And I've been working a long time at finding the old me again."

"You will," he said encouragingly.

But her heart felt heavy. "Some days I don't know if I will. Something changed that can't be fixed. So now I'm trying to create a new me—with the old parts that I miss but with the wisdom I've gained."

"That can only be a good thing, right?"

He should be right. Finding herself but being older and wiser sounded wonderful. But there was the small issue of forgiving herself, too. She hadn't quite nailed that yet. Living with the consequences seemed an appropriate penance most of the time. It ensured she'd never let the same thing happen again.

"The problem is with the wisdom comes the fear. And

trying to put it all together is really, really confusing. I hope one day I find the right balance. All I know is that from now on, I make my own decisions. The only person I'll depend on for happiness is me."

He reached across the table and laid his hand across hers. "You are one of the bravest women I've ever met. It'll happen for you. After all, there's no timetable, is there?"

She squeezed his fingers and then withdrew her hand before anyone saw them joined on the table top. Besides, she'd liked the feeling of them a little too much. "I'm getting impatient these days," she murmured. "Which I think is a good thing. The idea of moving forward is sounding really great."

"But Dad…"

"I told Molly I'll stay on as long as she needs me."

"And then?"

She shrugged. "I'll have to find another nursing job."

She toyed with her pie. Finding another job didn't hold a lot of appeal at the moment.

"So why did you become an LPN?"

Why had she? She supposed it had to do with growing up poor. She'd wanted to be a chef for a while. But cooking was something you did at home for your family, not a job. Working for minimum wage in a grocery store bakery wasn't a career plan, and whenever she'd mentioned cooking school her mother had flipped. It cost too much. The shorter Licensed Practical Nurse course was what they could afford, but Clara had felt suffocated. She figured that skipping town with Jackson was her way of rebelling. She'd only traded one prison for a much worse one.

"It was practical," she replied stiffly.

"But do you like it?"

She nodded. "Oh, I do. It wasn't my first choice, but

I like helping people. Seeing a patient's progress some-times…"

She stopped, realizing she was about to say too much. She picked up her tea and took a sip instead.

Ty tackled his sandwich, scooping up a forkful of bread, gravy and peas. "What about a patient's progress?" he asked, popping the food into his mouth.

She avoided his gaze, instead working on scraping some toasted coconut off the top of her pie. "Sometimes see-ing a patient improve was the brightest spot in my day."

Ty's leg brushed hers under the table. She looked up, startled, but his eyes were steady on hers. It was a very deliberate touch, but one that was away from anyone's curious eyes. Every nerve ending in her body stood to at-tention. It did not make her feel small or heavy with dread of what was coming next. It was, she realized, comfort-ing and reassuring. How did he, with no effort at all, ac-complish what no one else had accomplished in all these months?

"You realize those days are gone now, right?" His voice was quiet and his knee rubbed hers. "No one is going to hurt you here, Clara. I promise."

She couldn't look at him. If she did she'd blush and lose any coherent thoughts she was scrambling to put together in her head. It wasn't just that she liked how Ty's leg had felt. The simple thing would be to say that she was afraid of it, but that wasn't true either.

"Thank you," she said, her voice coming out sounding a bit strangled.

"I know the rumor mill says I'm a little wild…"

"A little?" she answered quickly, then put her fingers over her mouth. "I'm sorry. That wasn't fair."

His jaw tightened. "You're here to help Dad, and I don't want anything weird between us to get in the way of that.

That's all. I do want it to be better and right now you're one of the closest people to him. And you don't have the kind of bias that Mom does, because you don't have the history with the family. I'm not trying to come on to you, okay? It's not like that."

Of course it wasn't. The tingly feelings she felt were hers alone. Ty wasn't the least bit interested in her. He resumed eating his dinner while her hunger for pie seemed to disappear.

"Does the *wild* label bother you?" she asked, chancing another look up at his face.

He grinned. "I earned it fair and square."

Oh, that smile was lethal. For a second Clara stayed silent until curiosity got the better of her. "So why did you earn it? It sounds like you did it on purpose."

One eyebrow raised and he cupped his long fingers around his water glass. "You probably never did anything to rebel," he replied. "You seem perfectly nice and like…I don't know, like you always do what you should. I wasn't like that. I acted out. Molly should be a candidate for sainthood."

"If you're as stubborn as your father, then I agree." She smiled, but the grin was wiped from Ty's face.

"I never knew my real father," he replied flatly. "I've always said I got my wild streak from my mother and the Diamond stubbornness from Virgil. I really never stood a chance. Funny, I'm probably more Diamond than Sam is—son of one and raised by another—but it's me who's the black sheep."

"I can't imagine Molly and Virgil treating you as less than their own," she contradicted. "They seem very generous and fair and loving."

He shrugged. "I don't expect you to understand. You weren't dropped on a doorstep, Clara, because you weren't wanted by either of your parents. I'll never understand how she could do that. I don't plan on having kids of my own, but you can bet that if I did I'd do a lot better by them than mine did for me. My only link to them is biology. I don't even know if either of them is still alive."

He pushed away his plate. "Molly and Virgil are the only parents I've known. Without them I would have ended up in foster care. Once I graduated I left rather than disappoint them further. Rather than argue all the time."

"We all have choices," Clara responded, intrigued now at Ty's choice of words. Sometimes he called Molly and Virgil by their given names, and other times as Mom and Dad. But she noticed he never called him Uncle Virgil, even though his mother was Virgil's sister. "We just don't always choose the right thing," she added.

"Well, I'd like to do the right thing now. I've been studying the operation and I have ideas on expanding a certain area—and ideas on how to staff it. But I know he's going to tell me I'm crazy and we're going to argue again."

"So why not just put it on hold for a while? Go see him and say hello. Just talk, Ty. Surely there are good memories you can share and laugh over. Start there and see what comes of it. But don't stop trying."

She looked down at her plate, realizing that not trying was exactly what she'd done with her own family. "Maybe I'll even write *my* mom a letter. I haven't exactly been the model daughter."

"You? I can't imagine you doing anything wrong."

Clara pushed away her pie plate. "Oh, Ty." She sighed. "I followed the wrong man even after she told me I was making a huge mistake. And how does a daughter call up her mother and tell her that she's in the hospital because that man has beaten her? How does she say that she went back to that same man over and over?" Her throat tightened. "By the time it got to the point where I could say I found the courage to leave, it was too late, you know?"

This time Ty wasn't circumspect; he reached over and cupped her jaw in his hand. "If it's not too late for me, it's not too late for you." His thumb rubbed against her cheekbone. "I'll make you a deal. I'll try if you will, okay?"

She nodded, the rough texture of his hand oddly soothing against the soft skin of her cheek. "I think that's a good idea."

He withdrew his hand and she was surprised to find she missed the warmth of it.

"Let me look after this and I'll take you home," he said. He leaned forward to get his wallet out of his back pocket and Clara watched how the shape of his muscles beneath his shirt changed with the movement. He took some bills from his wallet, put them on the table, and reached for his jacket hanging on the back of his chair. Even in a cotton shirt, Clara could see there was not a spare ounce of flesh on him anywhere. Her mouth went dry as he shrugged into the coat and pulled up the zipper.

"You coming?" he asked.

"Oh, sorry," she replied, embarrassed at being caught staring. She reached for her coat and was again surprised when Ty took it from her hands and helped her put it on. She hadn't expected him to have such manners. "Thanks," she murmured, putting her purse over her shoulder.

Outside he opened her car door first before jogging around the hood and getting inside.

His chivalry made it feel like a date. Only most of the guys she'd dated hadn't bothered with the niceties either. "You don't have to do that stuff, you know," she said, folding her hands in her lap.

"What stuff?" He put the car in gear and headed out of

the parking lot. It was fully dark now and the headlights lit a swath ahead of them.

"You know. The coat and the car door."

He shrugged. "You've met my mother, right? She'd brain me if I didn't use my manners."

"You're nearly thirty." Clara chuckled as the image of the gentle Molly braining anyone was comical.

"I learned at a young age." He laughed, then sobered. "You asked me a while ago about being wild. I guess I was, but I always try to be upfront and honest. I never make promises I don't intend to keep. I always try to treat people with respect."

"Even the buckle bunnies?" She felt quite daring bringing up such a thing, but Ty was turning all of her preconceptions upside down.

He frowned. "Even them. Don't worry, Clara. They got exactly what they were after. They weren't looking to fall in love and neither was I. Everything upfront and mutual." He angled her a dry look. "And nowhere near as often as people would like to think."

What was it her mother had called her? A danger magnet? Sitting in Ty's muscle car in the dark made her feel just that. He had this edginess about him that was exciting, and yet this penchant for honesty and chivalry that added to the pull.

He pulled up in front of Butterfly House and put the car in park, where it idled with a throaty purr.

"And so what about me?" she asked. There'd been a push-pull thing going on ever since the wedding. "Are you honest with me?"

He turned in the seat slightly so he could look at her. His face was partially lit by the dashboard lights, creating light and shadow along the angles of his cheekbones and jaw. Her heart began beating erratically. How had she gotten here? Only a few short months ago she'd been a scared little mouse. Now she was sitting with Ty in his car in the dark asking him about his intentions.

Scary, but oh, it felt gloriously normal!

"I'm especially honest with you," he said, his voice low and intimate. "You scare the hell out of me, Clara."

It should have driven them apart and broken the spell, but it did exactly the opposite. The air felt warmer and the interior of the car smaller as she watched his tongue wet his lips.

"Me? Scare you?" Her words came out on a squeak.

"I don't know how to act around you. You're different. You've been through stuff I can't understand. I never know if I'm going to make things better or create a disaster. If I mess up or do something wrong, remember I'm trying to do the right thing."

"The right thing," she echoed.

He nodded slowly. "Yes. The right thing." He sighed. "I'm trying to do the right thing for everybody, so I'm bound to screw it up somehow."

Clara fought the urge to reach over and touch his thigh. He was being terribly open, wasn't he? She was starting to realize that beneath the sexy rebel was someone who cared very deeply. Who was kind.

Which made him an even worse sort of trouble.

He cleared his throat. "And now the right thing is for you to get out of the car and go inside and get a good night's sleep."

Clara clutched her purse. With a start she realized how easily he could have leaned over and kissed her. And more shock as she realized she would have let him.

She would have let Ty Diamond kiss her without a second thought.

"You're right," she said, sounding slightly breathless

as she put her hand on the door handle. "Thanks for the pie, Tyson."

"I'll come by in the morning to pick you up."

Nerves bubbled through her. She couldn't let herself get too familiar with him, or start relying on him either. "Don't worry about it. I'll have one of the girls run me over before they go to work."

"You sure?"

Oh, she was sure. She didn't want the added complication. She already cared for Molly and Virgil far more than she expected. She didn't want to come to care for him, too. Despite Molly's assurances, she knew this job wasn't permanent. She knew there was a new life out there for her, and one that didn't include Ty.

He said he tried to do the right thing. She had to, too.

"Good night," she said firmly, and climbed out of the car. It took all she had not to run to the front door, but she put one foot carefully in front of the other, methodically took her keys out of her purse and unlocked the door.

She didn't hear him drive away until she was inside with the door safely locked again.

CHAPTER FIVE

Ty STOOD OUTSIDE HIS father's room. He'd been there for a few minutes already, wondering if he was crazy to even try to talk to Virgil about his plans. But the past few days had been rather peaceful, making him think that perhaps Virgil would be open to new ideas. Besides that, Sam was due back from his honeymoon tomorrow. And Sam had already given his approval to at least assess Diamondback's operation and capacity for a different sort of expansion. Ty was ready to talk to him about moving forward.

But he had to talk to Virgil first. Without the old man feeling as if the boys were ganging up on him.

"You gonna stand out there all day?"

Virgil's strong voice made Ty jump, and he pushed the door open as if answering a command. "Dad."

"Something's on your mind if you stand outside my door that long." Virgil pushed himself up in bed so he was sitting, and gave Ty an assessing eye. "Bad news, eh?"

Great. This was not how Ty had planned to introduce things—on the back foot.

"Not at all." He went forward and pulled up a chair close to the bed. "I came in for a cup of coffee and thought I'd check in."

Virgil laughed, and Ty appreciated the rusty sound. It didn't happen enough around here. "Don't kid a kidder,

Ty. You haven't just 'checked in' on me since you got back. What's on your mind?"

"Sam's back tomorrow." There was no use mincing words now. Virgil was mostly bedridden but just as perceptive as ever. "I wanted to talk to you about something before he got back. To get your opinion."

His stomach twisted in knots. Undoubtedly Virgil's opinion would be that Ty was crazy. But Ty had promised Clara to try. He knew this was the right way even if he dreaded the outcome.

"Well, this is a change. You wanting my opinion on anything."

Ty refused to be provoked. "You might be surprised," he replied mildly. "We don't often see eye to eye, but I always valued your opinion. Even when I wished it came in the form of support. Which it rarely did."

How was that for honesty then?

Virgil fixed him with a beady eye, but Ty refused to squirm. They were grown men. Ty wasn't a boy any longer.

"So what hair-brained scheme are you cooking up this time?"

Ty considered the words he'd practiced. If he told Virgil the truth—that he wanted to work with an organization to provide employment to disadvantaged people—he knew what Virgil would say. That Diamondback hadn't become prosperous by being a charity. No, he had to come at it from a business perspective. Solid dollars and cents.

"Nothing hair-brained. I'd like to make a few adjustments, that's all. With Sam and I both back home, we can share the workload."

"Sam and I shared the workload and we didn't have a lot of spare time on our hands," Virgil argued.

But Ty was thirty and healthy and Virgil was in his seventies and slowing down. Ty wanted to point it out but didn't. "I've got nothing but time. Sam has Angela, but I'm commitment-free and ready to put my energy into Diamondback."

"Why now?"

Ty met his gaze evenly. "Why not?"

A reluctant chuckle wheezed from Virgil's throat. "You're just as stubborn as ever."

"I learned from the best," Ty returned. And smiled. They might knock heads over issues but there wasn't a man on earth he had more respect for than his father. Why else would he have tried so hard? Living up to Virgil's expectations had been impossible, but it didn't stop the gratitude. Or the love. If it had, maybe he wouldn't have felt the need to leave rather than face the hurt of being a constant disappointment.

"So you want to expand. How?"

"I want to add some quarter horses for one thing. Sam's biogas plant is making Diamondback greener. We've got the room to keep some good stock in the north barn and put them to good use around here. A lot of ranchers are blending old methods with new technology to make their operations more sustainable." He smiled. "Besides, I like working with horses. I'm good at it. We can add some to our own stock and I can train others into solid working stock—there's a market for it. And I can manage that part alone."

Virgil frowned. "We're a beef ranch. Sam's got this biogas thing going on and now you want to branch into horses. Do you even have any experience in training? What do you think is going to happen to beef production if you boys don't focus?"

Ty sighed. Perhaps Virgil didn't understand that Ty had spent a good many years working at operations big and small. He'd seen what worked and what didn't. "Nothing will be taken away from the beef, Dad. This is all going to make the operation better and more efficient. Diamondback beef is the best in the province, and our reputation is growing. We're working towards reaching sustainability standards so we can have official designation. For Pete's sake, everything Sam and I want to do is to make the ranch bigger and better by looking after the right things. Our priorities are bang on."

Virgil looked away. "You think you have all the answers. You always did."

"Maybe I wasn't always wrong," Ty said quietly.

Virgil said nothing.

"I came here to ask your opinion, whether you think so or not." Ty knew he couldn't possibly bring up the next idea today. Virgil was already riled up with this small little shift. "Is the focus your only concern?"

"How do you plan to pay for the new stock and what goes with it?"

Ty fought the urge to remind his father that Diamondback was a multi-million dollar operation. It had become that way because Virgil had always been diligent about dollars and cents, and Ty knew that in the beginning there had been lean times. He knew what the Diamond family had been. He'd heard the story of his mother often enough. Each time it had stung like a slice of a blade. He was the bastard Diamond. Left on a doorstep for all intents and purposes. He'd felt like a charity case a good portion of the time.

So it was with a fair amount of pride that he straightened his shoulders and said, "Out of my own pocket."

Virgil's lips fell open briefly before he raised an eyebrow. "Your money?"

"That's right."

"What money?"

Ty's temper started to simmer. "Money I earned. You know very well I haven't had a red cent from Diamondback since I left."

"I never cut you off."

Ty bit his tongue. No, Virgil never had. But Ty had refused any help when he walked away, determined to succeed on his own. To prove he could.

"I can finance whatever needs financing," Ty repeated. "If that's what you're getting at."

"How much?"

"I made some good investments." He didn't want to bring this down to a dollar value. Truth was, he'd lived simply and was fairly comfortable when all was said and done. His answer seemed to have momentarily silenced his dad. He wasn't sure if he was supposed to feel gratified at surprising Virgil, or if he was let down because he knew his dad expected so little of him.

"If you want to stop me, you're going to have to get out of that bed," he said, far more confidently than he felt on the inside. "Stop giving Clara the sharp side of your tongue and put your effort into your rehab."

"Clara hasn't complained." There was a note of petulance in Virgil's voice that made Ty want to smile. Virgil knew very well he'd been a grumpy old bear lately.

"Because she's too nice," Ty replied. He put his hands on the arms of the chair and boosted himself up. "She cares about you. Just because she's on the payroll doesn't mean she deserves your sass." He grinned suddenly. "Save it for me. I can take it. I have years of experience."

Virgil lifted his chin. "Hmm. There may be some Diamond in you after all."

"More than you'd like to think," Ty said, heading for the door.

"Tyson."

He turned around. Virgil had spun about on the bed. There was a wheelchair to one side and a walker on the other. The old man needed to get up and around again. Ty would take all the sharp remarks in the world if it meant Virgil was back to his old self once more.

Virgil nodded. "You and Clara. Are you, ah…"

The question made something funny turn in Ty's chest, something he was afraid to examine too closely. "No," he said. "We're not. She deserves a lot better man than me."

"For once we agree," Virgil replied, but for the first time there was no animosity in the words. Instead there was a camaraderie, the warmth of a shared joke. He was smiling at Ty, and Ty couldn't help but smile back.

"I have a ranch to run," Ty said gruffly. "Until you get off your ass and put me out of a job."

The best sound in the world was the sound of Virgil's laughter following him down the hall.

Things had gone better than he'd dared to hope. But what would Virgil say when he outlined his whole plan?

Clara saw the light on in the north barn and stared at it out the living room window for a few minutes. For the past few days the tension in the house had eased a bit. Virgil had apologized for his dark moods, Ty and Virgil actually sat at the dinner table without arguing, and now Sam and Angela were home and busy finishing the interior of their house, claiming that their do-it-yourself approach to decorating had sentimental value. Their arrival home at Diamondback had prompted a spur-of-the-moment celebration and Clara had been included in the family event. It had been bittersweet, feeling like she belonged and yet somehow knowing she didn't. The warmth, the laughter were all things she was starting to remember about being a part of a family and she missed it horribly.

The fact that her letter to her mother had come back undeliverable only made her feel more down.

Now Sam and Angela had gone home, Molly was in with Virgil, reading while he did a puzzle, and all that waited for her was the sunny yellow room at Butterfly House. Only a few months ago she'd been thrilled to move in there. Now it felt restrictive and, well, not like a home. She often found herself looking for ways to avoid it. What she really wanted was her own place.

But that would have to wait another month. In her pocket was the money to pay Ty back for her car parts. She should have done it before now, but she'd held off, trying not to touch her savings while waiting for payday.

She stared at the light a few moments more before grabbing a sweater and heading out the back door. She paid her debts. And she didn't want to owe Ty anything. He'd been absolutely perfect since the night at the diner. Their conversations had been pleasant and platonic. He'd stopped avoiding the house and came in for a coffee fill-up or simply to check in with Virgil.

But there were times—oh, catch-your-breath times— when their eyes met and she felt that butterfly sensation low in her stomach.

No, she didn't want to owe Ty Diamond anything.

The air was crisp but without the frosty bite that had been present earlier in the week. Her shoes crunched on the gravel of the drive as she made her way to the barn. She pushed the door aside and was greeted by warmth and the pungent but pleasant smell of horses. One whickered softly as she passed by the stalls, heading towards the beam of light slicing across the floor.

She found Ty in a small room. He'd fashioned a desk out of an old table and retrieved a rolling chair from somewhere, using an old wood box as a makeshift file drawer.

His head was bent over a notebook and papers were scattered over the top of the table. A calculator sat by his elbow.

She watched him for a few seconds. Something warm and tender wound its way through her insides. She'd never seen a man work harder than he did. Even with Sam home now, Ty worked from dawn until dusk. He reached for the calculator, punched in a few numbers and frowned. He rubbed a hand over his head—devoid of both ball cap and cowboy hat. The sable strands stood up on end in a careless mess.

In a million years she would not have expected this. She was beginning to care for Tyson Diamond. It was easy to dismiss the good looks and charm, but there was more to him than that. She'd seen it at the diner and she saw it every day. He tried. With the ranch, with his dad. And she'd bet he never thought he was up to scratch either.

"Hey," she said softly.

His head snapped up in surprise, and her heart did a little thump as he smiled at her. He leaned back in his chair and stretched. Her mouth went dry seeing his long arms extend to the side and the hollow of his throat extended. He let out a breath and rolled his shoulders. "Hey yourself. What are you doing out here?"

She found her wits and reached into her pocket. "I came to pay you back for the parts," she said, handing over the folded bills. "I'm sorry it took so long."

She really hoped he accepted it. She didn't want to start a whole "don't worry about it" thing where she felt indebted to anyone. He rubbed his thumb over the end of the bills and considered. Then he tucked it into his shirt pocket. "No problem. Car working all right?"

"Like a top."

He rested his elbows on the table. "Why do people say

that? Tops spin around and around unpredictably, then fall down."

He was in a lazy humor tonight and Clara found she liked it. "Like a dream, then?"

"Dreams are good," he replied, and tingles ran down her arms at the sound of his smooth, deep voice. There was not a soul out here with them in the barn. It was incredibly intimate. What was surprising was that she hadn't even had a second thought about being out here with him. She hadn't required a public situation for support. She hadn't needed a buffer between them. Goodness, she trusted him, didn't she? And other than Angela, she hadn't truly trusted anyone in years.

She blinked past the sting at the backs of her eyes. Ty would never understand the significance of this moment. But she did. It was another huge step in healing. It had begun the night he held her in his arms at the wedding dance.

"Are you all right?" Ty's voice broke through her thoughts and she smiled a wobbly smile.

"I'm great." She desperately wanted to move to another subject, so she waved a hand at the walls. "Sharing your office with a storeroom?"

Ty pushed his chair back. "The cupboards hold a lot of the medical supplies and various treatments we use around here. All it took was shifting a few boxes and I had my own office." He pointed at the floor to a small space heater. "Heat in the winter." He moved his thumb so it pointed at a window. "Air conditioning in summer."

She leaned against the doorjamb. "You could probably set up an office in the house, you know. Molly wouldn't mind and even Virgil seems to be getting used to you these days."

"Here," he said, getting up and retrieving a wooden

crate from the corner and setting it on its end. "Have a seat."

She perched on the crate and folded her hands. Ty sat back down in his chair. The seat was slightly higher than her box so she still had to tilt her head a bit to look into his face. He looked tired, she realized.

"I like it out here," he explained. "If what I want to do actually happens, I'll be making this into an actual office. My own piece of Diamondback, you know?"

"Is this about the horses, then?"

He shrugged. "Partly. There's more to it, but one step at a time. We've got all the facilities right here. We're just not using them. Besides, Sam's the cattle man. I know he plans on helping Angela with the foundation, but beef will always be his baby and that's as it should be." He crossed an ankle over his knee. "Why shouldn't I have something of my own?"

Clara understood that. After all, she had taken this job as a stepping stone to a new life. "I know what you mean," she replied. "Don't get me wrong, I've loved working here. Molly and Virgil have been so good to me. And Angela's foundation—I don't know where I'd be without it. But I want something of my own, too. I've spent years following. I followed Jackson. And when my life blew up I followed what everyone told me I had to do. Now it's time for me to have something for me. I think I'm ready for that."

"Good for you," he said warmly. "You deserve it, Clara."

Silence spun out for a few moments and Clara realized she should get going. Ty showed no signs of stopping work and it probably wasn't the wisest thing to stay out here alone for too long. "Anyway," she said, standing up, "I should get back. Tomorrow's another day, right?"

Ty pushed back his chair. "I'll walk you out. I could stand to give my legs a stretch."

They ambled their way down the barn corridor, their steps slowing more and more as the door drew closer. The horses were quiet now in the dark with only the soft sounds of the odd hoof or snuffle breaking the silence. With only the slightest shift Clara knew her shoulder could be touching his arm. If she reached out the tiniest bit, her fingers would brush with his. They were silly thoughts. Why would Ty want to hold her hand? They weren't shy teens anymore. They weren't even really interested in each other, were they?

They were nearly to the door now and it seemed every nerve ending Clara possessed was on high alert. She *was* interested in Ty. She thought about him far too often and she was way too aware of him. But that wasn't the same thing as being interested in a relationship. They were two very different things. Attraction was momentary. Relationships represented a commitment too scary to even really comprehend.

But it didn't stop the tingling sensations she felt as his arm brushed hers, sliding the barn door a few feet to the side, letting in a chilly puff of air.

"The moon's bright tonight," Ty murmured. His body blocked the door part way; there was no way she could slip through the gap without brushing against him. She swiped her tongue over her lips that seemed suddenly dry.

"It was full two nights ago," she replied, closing her eyes briefly as she realized how breathy she sounded.

"But cloudy." Ty still didn't move. He pointed upwards. "Look. It's so clear the stars go on forever. The unending sky is my favorite thing about the prairies."

She moved forward a bit but her view was blocked by the breadth of Ty's chest. He slid back against the heavy wood frame of the doorway, making room for her to peer through.

The sky was enormous and stunning, full of twinkling stars and the steady, watchful gaze of planets. A cloud of breath frosted the view for a moment as she tilted her head up to watch a satellite cross the sky in a steady, perfect arc.

"What do you suppose it's watching?" she whispered, pointing at the moving dot.

When Ty didn't answer, she turned her head. He wasn't watching the stars at all. Instead he was looking at her. He wasn't smiling. But there was something about him that made her forget the fall air and made her warm all over.

"Look at the stars," she chided softly. "They're beautiful."

"No more beautiful than you."

Her breath caught in her chest, making it difficult to breathe.

"Why did you really come out here tonight?"

She couldn't answer. Instead she bit down on her lip as she stayed suspended in the delicious sensation of being the sole focus of Ty's attention.

He lifted his hand and rested it on the side of her neck while his thumb brushed the curve of her jaw. Breathing was torturous now as Ty's face seemed to come closer. His eyes were open—those gloriously velvet eyes with gold flecks dancing around his pupils. The cotton of his shirt touched the knit of her sweater as their bodies drifted closer.

But Clara was totally lost when he raised his other hand and cradled her face in his palms, as if he was holding something precious and fragile. There was no fear here. No hesitation. There was no darkness, only light.

"Clara," he murmured, and he shifted his head the tiniest bit, closing the remaining gap and touching his lips to hers.

Her lips drifted closed as the sensation rippled through her. His lips were soft and gently persuasive. Instinctively hers parted beneath his, willingly yet carefully tasting what he was offering. What she discovered was sweetness. She hadn't expected sweetness from a man like Ty.

His hands moved from her face to cup her neck, his fingers tangling with her hair, moving through her curls but demanding nothing. All her preconceptions drifted away on the night air. He was the Cadence Creek bad boy. She'd expected him to take. But he wasn't. He was giving, and she rested a trembling hand on his chest for balance as she tilted her head and leaned into the kiss.

He was a solid wall of muscle and man, steady and strong. As she slid her hand up to his shoulder the kiss deepened, losing a touch of its sweetness and replacing it with a wildness that was a promise of what lay ahead. It was an urgency that was somehow unrushed—an acknowledgement of the flare of passion without the need to let it burn out.

It was the most incredible kiss she'd ever experienced.

Ty broke away first, resting his forehead against hers for a few seconds. His breath fanned her cheek in small gasps and she felt the accelerated rise and fall of his chest and shoulders beneath her fingers.

The last thing she expected to see when she pulled back and looked into his face was concern.

"Are you okay?" he asked quietly. "I didn't mean to push. To rush you. I…"

Emotion rushed through her veins—relief and gratitude and affection and awe. She stood on her tiptoes and put her arms around his neck, drawing him into a hug.

"Hey," he soothed, but he didn't push her away. He

looped his arms around her back and rubbed the base of her spine. "It's okay. Right?" His breath was warm on her hair. "Should I have asked first?"

He sounded so unsure. It was a revelation, and a smile blossomed on her lips. She nodded against his neck. "It's okay," she said, the words muffled but discernible. He tightened his arms around her and she wanted to weep with the wonder of it. It was more than a kiss between them. He knew. He understood.

She let him go and tried to get herself together. The last thing she wanted was to cry all over his shirt. He would think she was upset but really it was just a lot of bottled-up emotion that needed to come out. She ran her finger under her lashes and took a big breath. When she could look at him without tears, she met his gaze.

"Thank you, Ty. I…" Her voice caught and she swallowed. "I was so afraid I'd never be able to…to…" She didn't know how to explain the hesitation and fear that had been a part of her life for so long.

"Shh," he said, and to her surprise he turned her by the shoulders and circled her with his arms, so her back was nestled against his chest. "Just look up there for a minute, and breathe."

The stars glittered, perhaps a little brighter than before, as she rested her head against the indent where his shoulder met his chest. His hands rested against the thick waistband of her sweater and she covered them with her own. For several minutes they stood that way, watching the inky sky and the shifting constellations.

"Do you know," he whispered in her ear, "that in the winter, when the conditions are just right, you can see the Northern Lights from here?"

"I've never seen them," she whispered back.

"Maybe you'll be able to this winter," he suggested.

Clara felt a sudden chill. This winter? But she wouldn't
be here, would she? At some point Virgil would be able to
make do with the extramural nurse a day or two a week,
or a drive into town for a physio session. She would be
leaving Diamondback behind. She'd be leaving them *all*
behind.

She stepped out of his embrace. This had been amazing, wonderful, but it wasn't real, was it? It wasn't practical or advisable. If she kept going on the way she was
going she would end up hurt.

"I really should be getting back, Ty. It's getting late."

"I'll walk you to your car."

"You don't have to."

"Yes, I do."

He waited while she grabbed her purse from the kitchen
and then walked beside her to her car. When she got there
he put his hand on the door handle to open it, but hesitated.
When she met his gaze, he stepped forward and kissed her
again. Without the breathless hesitation of the last time. It
was soft but deliberate. And sexy as hell.

He stood back, opened the door and held it.

Her cheeks flared with heat. Her body hummed with the
sense of him—his scent, the feel of him, his taste. "This
isn't a good idea, Tyson."

He smiled in the dark. "I knew you were going to say
that."

"Not that it wasn't...you know," she continued awkwardly. "Surprising."

"And good?"

Damn him. "And good," she admitted.

"But?"

She sighed. "Yes, but. Tonight was a big step for a girl
like me. I haven't allowed myself to be close to anyone,
Ty. I felt safe with you. Don't ruin that, please."

His smile turned to a scowl. "You think I'll ruin it?"

She shook her head. "You won't mean to. But we both know this can't go anywhere. You have too much on your plate right now, and I'm going to be moving on. We both know this is temporary. I don't belong here. It's just my job. I care about your family but one day soon I'll have a new job, very likely in a new place. I'm going to build my own life. Getting involved any further would only complicate things."

She put her hand on the car door. "Ty, I'm trusting you to understand when I say that I can't handle complications on top of everything else in my life right now."

"You're not ready."

"I'm not ready," she confirmed. "And that's not the kind of girl for you. You need someone confident and sure of herself, not someone who needs to be fixed. That's not fair to you. Or to me."

"I'm not sorry it happened."

She wanted to reach out and touch him so badly. But she had to be strong. She couldn't send mixed messages anymore. "I'm not sorry either," she murmured. "But it has to end here."

Ty nodded. "Let's just take a step back, okay? Get the ground beneath us again."

Clara nodded, but the bubble of elation from earlier had popped, leaving a thread of unease trickling down her spine. Why did she get the feeling that Ty wasn't going to back off as easily as he said?

Her feelings for Ty had snuck up on her and she couldn't deny they were real. But as she shut the car door and started the engine, she pressed a hand to her abdomen, against an invisible pain. It couldn't go further than tonight. She didn't want to count on someone again. She didn't want to go through losing someone again. And she definitely didn't want the despair of her dreams being destroyed one more time.

Never again.

CHAPTER SIX

OCTOBER'S BRISK, GOLDEN days turned to the gray days of November. The snow still held off, the clouds spitting out random flakes now and then. The days got shorter, and Ty woke most mornings in the dark and then ate his dinner in the dark at night.

It was not his favorite time of year.

Clara still came and went from the house, and Ty tried to keep things on an even keel with her—at least on the outside. He hadn't meant to kiss her that night. Hadn't meant to hold her in his arms. Hell, after their dance he knew she was skittish as a new colt. And she had a good reason.

But he'd been thinking about her too much. And she'd appeared in his cubby hole of an office, all wide blue eyes and wearing that thick, completely unsexy sweater like body armor, holding out money that he wanted to tell her to put back in her pocket.

He turned up his collar against the wind and nudged Strawberry forward, holding the reins loosely in his gloved hand. The mare hadn't had much exercise lately and he'd decided to give her a treat with a ride out to the west butte. It had given him time to think, too. He'd been putting off really talking to Virgil for days. Ty had known all along that he could finance his project on his own. Sam had loved the idea. No, it was one tiny detail that kept sticking to Ty like a burr under a saddle. He was afraid of disappointing Virgil once more.

He took Strawberry into the barn, removed her saddle and bridle and gave her a good rubdown before turning her out in the paddock. The fresh air had worked up his appetite, so he thought a cup of coffee and a slab of the marble cake Molly had whipped up yesterday might hit the spot.

The house was quiet inside, but the coffee was hot in the pot. He poured a cup and cut a slice of cake, standing over the kitchen sink to eat it. Crumbs dropped into the stainless steel sink as he looked out over the barnyard. It was good to be back. He'd been gone a long time, but he was glad now that Sam had made the call and asked him to come home. This was where he belonged. Things would work out. They had to.

He turned from the sink and saw Clara's tote bag on the hook by the front door. He had no idea what to do about her. One part of his brain knew she was right—they both knew this was a temporary position and that she would be moving on. Another part of his brain reminded him that she'd been through hell and it was a lot for her—and a potential partner—to overcome. So he'd backed off like she'd asked.

The thing getting in the way was his heart. When he'd set foot back on Diamondback soil the last thing on his mind had been getting involved with a woman. Especially not a shy, buttoned-to-the-neck nurse with a wagonload of baggage as big as his own.

But there she'd been, right from the first night. And kissing her under the stars had unlocked something inside him. Something he suspected he'd been searching for for a long time. He didn't have to pretend to be someone else with Clara. He didn't have to put on a show or hide away.

His heart didn't want him to back away. His heart wanted him to hold on and he was having a heck of a time deciding exactly what he should do.

So as he finished up his coffee and wandered down the hall to his dad's room, he decided that he'd simply keep on as he had been—waiting. There was no rush, was there?

Virgil was making his way from the bathroom to his bed with the help of his walker. Was it just Ty or did the shuffling steps seem shorter than before? Clara was there beside him, quietly encouraging. As Ty appeared in the doorway she looked up and smiled. But before the smile he caught the shadow of concern in her eyes.

"Look who's come to see you," Clara said brightly as Virgil sat on the edge of the bed. "Just the person to drag you out of your doldrums."

"Dad," Ty said, stepping inside. He smiled at Clara and nodded. They were in this together. Clearly Virgil wasn't having a very good day and they were going to do their best to bring him around.

Maybe it wasn't the best time to talk about what was weighing on his mind after all.

"It looks like it's cold out," Virgil remarked as Clara helped him swing his legs over the mattress.

"It is. I took Strawberry out for a ride. Air's brisk. Maybe we'll have snow tonight."

The weather was a good place to start, right?

"Been thinking about what you said." Virgil let out a labored breath. "About the horses. If Sam's in agreement, I won't stand in your way."

Ty frowned. Just like that? Why was Virgil giving in so easily? Not that he wasn't pleased. But it wasn't like his father to back down. He'd expected more of a fight.

"I appreciate that. I've crunched some numbers and talked to Sam. I also thought I'd convert the storeroom in the barn into an office." He pulled the chair next to the bed closer and sat in it. "It's not fair to Sam, or to you, for me to tie this to Diamondback. Other than the space, this will stay completely separate from the cattle operation."

"You don't have to do that. I trust you."

Ty sat back in his chair, flummoxed. "You do?"

Virgil nodded.

Clara was quietly tidying up around the room. Ty wondered if this was the opening he'd been waiting for. With his heart in his throat, he reached for his father's hand and clasped it between his own.

"Then I should tell you about the rest, Dad."

One of Virgil's eyebrows went up. "There's more?"

Ty nodded. "I'm going to need to hire some help, some new hands. I've talked to Angela, who has agreed to make some connections for me. There are a lot of people out there who are stuck for one reason or another—a bad choice, a disability…people who haven't had the advantages I had. Some people who need a fresh start and someone to give them a chance." He swallowed and when he continued his voice was thick with emotion. "Where would I be now if you and Mom hadn't taken me in? I was lucky."

Virgil's eyes were wide. "If you were so lucky, then why did you leave?"

Clara was beside the door, ready to sneak out but Ty shook his head. "Stay," he said quietly. "I've got nothing to hide."

She hesitated, met his gaze. For a long moment he was remembering the feel of her in his arms as she'd hugged him. Why didn't he care if she knew the truth? He'd been so careful to keep it hidden for years.

Was he falling in love with her?

She took a chair across the room and picked up a ball of yarn and knitting needles. He watched the points flash

back and forth as she worked on something that was dark
gray with red stripes. Looking at her made him feel better. Calm rather than scattered. Settled.

He shook his head and turned back to his father. Falling in love was impossible. And right now he needed to
patch things up with his dad. Enough time had passed.
They had to make amends.

"I left because I always felt like I somehow disap-
pointed you. Like you wished I was more like Sam. Sam
was yours and I was the charity case."

"You were my son."

The plainly spoken words went straight to his heart.
"It didn't always feel that way. Sam always seemed to do
everything right. I idolized him. Heck—" he grinned suddenly "—I still do." The smile slid from his face. "And I
always felt like I fell just a little bit short of your expectations. I felt like a burden."

"Tyson."

"No, I need to say this. I heard you once," he continued. "When I was eight. I'd gotten in trouble at school for
fighting. You were talking to Mom and you said that you
hadn't even wanted to adopt me."

Virgil said nothing.

"I knew you didn't want me. I tried to earn my way
but the harder I tried the more I screwed up, and the more
I screwed up the more we argued, until I knew we were
going to go crazy. That's why I left. I couldn't stand disappointing you anymore."

Virgil had closed his eyes, but when Ty finished he
opened them. The dark depths were swimming in tears.
"Stupid boy," he murmured. "My sister did beg me to
adopt you. When she showed up and begged me to take
you, I resisted. I thought you'd be better off with her—
your real mother. But Molly saw what I didn't. That Junie

was an addict who'd gotten pregnant and was in no way ready to be a mother. I didn't want to believe it, but after you'd been here a week I knew we couldn't give you up. I never regretted it. Not even when you drove me crazy. What you heard was only part of the truth. I hadn't wanted to adopt you, but I was never sorry. I loved you even when you made it difficult."

Ty's heart expanded and he blinked back tears. In all his life he'd never heard Virgil say he loved him. "Then why did you push so hard? Why did you make me feel like such a failure?" The words came out as a hoarse whisper.

Virgil shook his head. "I never meant to, son. I only wanted you to grow up to be a good man. You already had baggage, knowing where you came from and the circumstances. I wanted you to be better than that. To be bigger than that. I wanted more for you than you thought you deserved. I could see the potential in you and you only seemed to throw it away. I had faith you could do better, even if you didn't think you were capable of it yourself. It was frustrating as hell to watch." Virgil finished talking and coughed.

"I didn't know that," Ty whispered, trying desperately to hold on to his emotions. Why hadn't they talked about this sooner? Why had it taken a call from Sam for Ty to finally come home? He swallowed around a lump in his throat. Stupid pride.

"I pushed too hard and I drove you away."

Virgil dropped his head and his chest shook. Ty hadn't truly thought his heart could break until that moment. He had never seen his father cry. Not ever. Virgil was a shadow of the strong man he'd used to be, reduced to being bedridden most of the time, frail and weak. And now Ty had made him cry.

He got up on the bed beside his father and put his arms

around him. "It's okay," he whispered. "I'm here now. We can fix it."

As he held his father he became incredibly aware how much smaller the big man had become during his illness. He lifted his eyes and looked over at Clara. She'd dropped her knitting into her lap, her hands resting on the forgotten needles and her eyes shimmered with tears. Ty fought the urge to wipe his away. He hated that she was seeing him this way, but he had to put his discomfort aside. For once, something was more important than the barrier he usually built around himself.

He squeezed Virgil's arm and cleared his throat. "Okay now, Dad?"

Virgil nodded. A tissue appeared by Ty's arm—Clara holding it out—and he took it and tenderly wiped the tears from Virgil's cheeks.

"We should have talked a long time ago," Ty decreed, still uncomfortable with all the emotion but somehow feeling lighter than he had in ages.

"Stubborn. You get that from the Diamonds," Virgil replied. When he smiled Ty noticed his mouth was still a little lopsided from the lingering effects of the paralysis.

"Who, me?" Ty looked back at the chair, expecting to see Clara, but she'd disappeared. It was just as well. She'd gotten an eyeful today and it definitely wasn't Ty at his best.

Virgil tried a laugh, but he began coughing again. "Here," Ty said. "Let's fix your pillows and get you a drink."

Once his father was settled Ty sat back in the chair. "About the staffing, Dad. I want to give people a chance. People aren't so different from animals, you know." He smiled. "They just need some dignity and encouragement.

I spent so long riding bulls and wandering around. It's time I did something really important. Something meaningful."

Virgil's gaze—still sharp despite everything—met Ty's. "Proud of you," he said with a sigh. He patted Ty's hand. "Proud of you."

"You should get some rest now." Ty got up and shoved his hands in his pockets. Now that they'd opened up, he felt awkward and oddly vulnerable. They'd patched things up, but somehow the heavy feeling of expectation remained. Ty knew he had to make his plan work. He couldn't fail. His father had put his faith in Ty, and Ty couldn't bear the thought of disappointing him again.

Clara finished washing out the mugs and placed them in the drying rack. Since Ty had talked to Virgil two days before, a change had come over the house. A peacefulness of sorts and a positive energy that had been missing. Molly was thrilled that Ty and Virgil had mended fences, Virgil had lost his ornery attitude, and Ty smiled more, which always put a glad feeling in Clara's heart.

So it made no sense whatsoever that she was on edge, with the uneasy feeling that something was horribly off. No matter how she tried, she couldn't shake the sense that something was wrong.

"Penny for your thoughts."

The mug she was holding slipped from her fingers and shattered on the ceramic tile of the kitchen floor.

"What the…" Ty stepped around the pieces of pottery and peered into her face. "I didn't mean to startle you. Are you okay?"

Heat rushed into her face. "I was just preoccupied. And feeling silly now. I'm fine. I'll just get the dustpan and clean this up."

"I'll get it." Ty went to the broom closet and pulled out

the broom and dustpan. "Sit down. You look as though you're ready to tip over."

She hadn't been sleeping, that was why. She worked all day and then went home and made sure she carried her weight at Butterfly House, taking her turn at laundry and meals and dishes according to the house schedule. She had started knitting some wool socks for Virgil to wear as the days got colder—anything to keep her hands busy and tire her out so she could sleep at night. But each night she lay awake. She couldn't stop thinking about Ty. About how it had felt to kiss him. About how afraid she was to care for him. And how the unfamiliar longings pulling at her lately were completely at odds with the plans she'd made.

She wished she'd never witnessed that conversation Ty had had with Virgil. She'd cared about him before. But she'd seen something more that afternoon that only made her more scared and confused.

"I can do it," she replied, hearing a snap in her voice she instantly regretted. She tempered her tone. "Don't mind me. I've just had a lot on my mind lately."

He waved her away and stooped to sweep the pieces into the dustpan. "So you said. Maybe you need some fresh air."

Deep down she knew what she needed. She needed to move on, find her own place, be independent. Here in Cadence Creek—at Diamondback—she was pulled away from what she knew was the best course for her. She was too personally involved. Yet how could she up and quit? Molly relied on her. So did Virgil. She'd feel as though she was abandoning them all.

It had nothing to do with missing Ty, she told herself. She told herself that a lot lately. And perhaps if she said it enough times it would be true.

"Maybe," she murmured, watching Ty dump the dust-pan in the garbage.

He put everything back in the broom cupboard and turned around. "I came in for my gloves. Why don't you bundle up and come with me? I've been trying to spend some time evaluating each of the horses. There's a gelding you could ride. He's an old fellow who is as calm as can be."

Clara hadn't been on a horse since she was a girl. And yet an hour outside in the fresh air sounded heavenly. "I'm pretty inexperienced," she said, "and I'd just slow you down."

He laughed. "It isn't a race. Besides, Herb needs some activity, too. You're perfect for each other."

"Herb?" She tried not to snicker, but failed.

Ty smiled, that secret, lopsided smile that made her go a little lightheaded each time she saw it. "Yes, Herb. He came to us years ago with the lofty handle of Conqueror. You'll understand when you see him."

"Well..."

"Don't 'well' about it. Put on your coat. Did you wear a hat?" She shook her head, but he was undeterred. "We'll grab one of Mom's, then. And you'll need gloves. It's brisk out there today."

She let herself be convinced because it really did sound like fun. She'd spent a long time doing what "needed" to be done, she'd taken barely any time for herself. She'd almost forgotten what fun was. The closest she'd come was pie at the diner with Ty. "Let me put on my boots," she replied. "I'll meet you in the barn."

CHAPTER SEVEN

SHE FOUND TY in the corridor with a gorgeous chestnut cross-tied. Ty hefted a saddle over the horse's back, swinging it as if it weighed nothing, centering it on the blanket and adjusting the position just a little. He wore his black cowboy hat and a brown jacket with a heavy collar. He was the very picture of a rugged cowboy, and for a moment Clara caught her breath. He was so strong and capable—far more than he gave himself credit for.

She finally found her tongue and stepped forward. "Is this Herb?"

Ty looked up, his face pressed against the horse's smooth hide as he tightened the cinch. "Of course not. This here is Rattler. Seven years old and too smart for his own good. A little too much horse for a greenhorn." He flashed her a quick smile. "No, that's Herb." He pointed his thumb towards another stall where a horse waited, tacked and ready to ride.

"Of course he is," Clara said, immediately understanding, and she let out a laugh on a delighted breath. His bones were too sound to be called a nag. But the dappled gray had a low-maintenance look. His wide eyes had a knowing look to them, his forelock hung shaggily down the center of his nose, and she smiled widely at the sight of one back hoof resting jauntily on its edge on the floor as if to say, "Whenever you're ready. Take your time." All in all he *looked* like a Herb—not a Conqueror at all!

"Can you lead him out?"

Clara reached over the stall door and rubbed Herb's nose. Sure she could do this. She stepped inside and grabbed the reins. "Come on, Herb."

His hooves made slow clopping sounds on the concrete—Herb wasn't one to hurry—and then they were outside, standing on the hard gravel while Ty followed with the high-stepping Rattler. Clara looked up into Herb's brown eyes. He looked trustworthy. Surely riding a horse was like riding a bike, right? Determined to take the initiative, she put her foot in the stirrup, grabbed hold of the saddle horn and none too gracefully hauled herself up, swinging her leg over the saddle before plopping down heavily in the seat. Herb looked around as if to say, "Hey, take it easy back there!"

She could hear Ty's light laughter behind her. "That's the spirit," he said, and moved closer to adjust her stirrups. She looked at Rattler, who had stopped his prancing and was standing quietly even without Ty's hands on the leather. Ty held his gloves in his teeth as his sure fingers adjusted the buckles until her boot was cushioned in the stirrup. When he was done, he slipped the gloves back on his hands, took Rattler's reins and then slipped into the saddle with the balletic grace of a dancer.

"Warm enough?"

She nodded, and then as an afterthought pulled the knitted hat down over her ears. It was a thick, mismatched hat and the green color clashed with the red of her coat, and she knew that she must look comical next to Ty's cowboy perfection. But today she was leaving her insecurities behind. In the sharp bite of the cold air and the wide-open prairie, what did it matter if she didn't match? If she were less than perfect? She'd needed this—to get out for a while. Shake off the cobwebs and swing her arms a bit.

"Let's go then," he said, and led the way at a leisurely walk.

For several minutes Clara was happy to ride beside Ty in silence. The ranch land spread out before them: brown, undulating fields that stretched on forever, broken only by the odd stand of trees or winding creek. The clouds were steel-gray and forbidding, but the rhythm of the horse's slow stride was comforting and the basics of riding came back to Clara without much trouble. She breathed deeply and let out the air, relaxing in the idea that for the foreseeable future the only thing she had to do was ride until Ty said to turn around and head back. Nothing could touch her out here. Not her painful past, not her worries about the future. Not the niggling feeling of dread she'd felt in the house lately. None of it mattered. The center of her universe was a man and his horse. She wondered if, in a different time and place, he might have been *her* man. Or if he could be now, if she were only brave enough to speak up?

Brave. Huh. She definitely wasn't that, and she wondered if she ever would be. No matter how much she found herself drawn to Ty, there was always something—that little bit of fear and uncertainty preventing her from taking a step forward. It was the pain, she realized. When she'd left Jackson there hadn't just been fear. There'd been pain over what she'd lost. There'd been blame, too, and feeling as though she'd let so many people down. And she simply couldn't find a way to get past how much it hurt. Maybe she never would.

When they reached the creek, Ty stopped and dismounted. "Might as well let them have a drink," he said, taking Herb's reins and holding him while she climbed out of the saddle. She already felt the impact of an hour astride in her thighs, and she gave her legs a little shake as she laughed.

"I'm very out of practice."

"You're doing fine. You looked like you needed some fresh air."

"I did." She chafed her hands together as Ty looped the reins around the saddle horn and let Herb wander to the creek alone. "You don't worry about him wandering away?"

Ty chuckled. "Not this guy. Or Rattler either. Especially if I take out the apples I have stuck in my pockets."

She smiled, but the silence that followed was awkward, as if they were waiting for the other to say something. Finally Ty spoke up.

"Clara, about the other day…"

She looked up and met his gaze. She was right. He was feeling uncomfortable.

"Why did you leave?"

She shrugged. "It seemed like it was a private moment between you and your father. I felt like I was intruding. And the two of you obviously needed it, Ty." She didn't mention that seeing the two of them had done something to her emotionally, something so strong that she'd had to retreat to a corner to shed her own tears. The men she'd known all her life had never shown their feelings like that. She hadn't known men could. Seeing Ty with his arms around Virgil, opening himself up to that vulnerability…

She swallowed.

"You heard what I plan to do then. My hiring plans?"

"I think it's wonderful." She tilted her head. "It just made me wonder…"

"Wonder what?"

Herb came back from the creek and, true to form, nuzzled his nose at Ty's pocket. Ty reached inside and took out an apple. He squeezed it in such a way that it broke in half, and he held out the first piece on his palm. Herb gathered it up in his lips and munched.

"Wonder why you hide the generous and compassionate man behind the facade of a…" She faltered. What was he exactly? Charming. A player? Perhaps at one time, but not now. She'd known him over a month and she had yet to even hear of him going on a date let alone playing the field. An egomaniac? Playboy? None of the names seemed to fit.

"A what?"

Herb nuzzled for the second half and Ty held it out mindlessly as he kept his gaze locked with hers.

"I don't know. You came back to Cadence Creek with this reputation. Of being a ladies' man. Of being cocky. The smooth rodeo star who says all the right things to make the women blush. But that's not you, is it?"

"No, it's not. It was just easier than being myself. Except when I'm with you…"

Her heart started pounding. "When you're with me?"

"I don't want to be that person. I feel like if I even tried it, you'd see right through me. It's a pain in the ass, to be honest. You've totally blown my cover."

She laughed and held out her hand for an apple. He took out another, split it, and gave her a piece. Rattler came over and she took off her glove, letting the apple sit on her open palm. The flesh and juice were cold and Rattler's lips were velvety soft against her skin. On impulse she lifted her hand and rubbed the horse's neck. The hair there was coarse but smooth.

Ty joined her, resting his palm against the firm hide. "Clara, I want to tell you the real reason why I wasn't at dad's seventieth birthday a few years back. He's never asked, and things are still pretty raw between us. I'll explain to him someday. But I want you to know, because of what you've been through. Because of what's happened between us."

The smile slipped from her lips. Ty was being terribly serious. "Okay."

"Let's walk," he suggested, snagging Herb's reins and handing them to her. They walked side by side as they led the horses away from the creek bank. Clara's boots crunched against the frosty blades of grass and she tucked her free hand into her pocket for extra warmth. The air had a bitter bite to it now, and she wondered if they weren't finally due for that snowfall.

"I spent a few nights in jail," he explained. "I was all set to come home. I'd told myself I'd hold my tongue and put on a pleasant face and show up for the old man. Mom had asked and even Sam called. I was planning on leaving and driving down, but I'd loaned something to one of the hands I was working with at the time. I drove by to pick it up—and interrupted something."

Something heavy seemed to settle in Clara's stomach. "What did you interrupt?"

"Him, trying to keep his wife in line."

The heavy weight did a sickening twist.

"What did you do?"

"Put him in line instead."

"Oh, Tyson."

He sighed. "I know what you're going to say. Violence doesn't solve other violence, right?"

"That's probably what I should be saying."

"But you're not?"

She shook her head. "No, I'm not." She hesitated for a second and then said, "There were so many times I wished someone would come in and give Jackson a taste of his own medicine. That they'd swoop in and rescue me. But I finally realized that it wasn't up to anyone else to rescue me. I had to do it for myself. For my…"

She halted, and Herb's hoof beats quieted.

"For your?"

She'd almost come right out and said it, hadn't she? The thing that only the doctors and the social workers knew. That she'd been pregnant during that final beating.

Ty somehow made her forget that she had any secrets left at all. This one was too close, too painful to share. She shook her head and resumed walking, Herb following obediently beside her. "Never mind. Tell me what happened after that."

Thankfully he let his question drop. "She called the police."

Clara's brow furrowed. "How did *you* end up in lockup then?"

He gave her a pointed look and she suddenly understood. "She called the police on you, not him."

"Right the first time."

Clara sighed. "I know it doesn't make sense, but it happens more often than you'd think. For so many complicated reasons, Ty. At least you tried to help."

"I'll admit I didn't make it easy for the officers. I didn't exactly go quietly. They put me in a cell to cool down. By the time I got out, it was too late to drive home for the party. Then I'd have to explain why I was late and also the condition of my face."

"The charges were dropped?"

"The next day there was a 9-1-1 call from the house. He'd taken my interference out on her. There wasn't much reason to keep me in jail. But I figured it was time I got out of Dodge. I quit and moved on to a new place outside Fort McMurray."

"So it looked like you were guilty anyway."

He shrugged. "I suppose it did."

"But Ty—" She stopped again, clutching the reins in her hand. "Surely you must have known your parents would understand. You were just standing up for someone."

He stopped, too. Stepped a foot closer and his face softened. He was looking at her almost tenderly, she realized, as the all-too-familiar thumping of her heart started again. He put his gloved palm against her face. It was cold and smelled like worn leather and horse. It was a scent she knew she'd always associate with him.

"Sweet Clara," he murmured, looking down at her. "Even after all you've been through, you look for the best in people. You accept them. I wish I had been more like you. Maybe I wouldn't have stayed away. Maybe I never would have left at all."

She stepped back, stunned. She considered herself distrusting at best, jaded at her worst. Cautious and careful. But Ty didn't see her that way. He saw her the way she'd always wanted to be but thought she fell short.

"But I'm so withdrawn," she replied, frowning. "Cold. I see it in myself and I wish I wasn't. You're wrong, Ty."

He shook his head. "I don't know how to explain it." He adjusted his hat on his head as if trying to shake up the right words. "You don't hold other people away from you. You hold yourself away from them. There's a difference."

It shouldn't have made sense but it did. She loved Molly, and Virgil, Angela and even Sam, she supposed. She felt affection towards them all. But he was right. She stopped just short of offering herself. She allowed them to welcome her in—she accepted them—but she didn't let them accept her in return.

"I'm sorry," she murmured.

"Don't be. I get it. Maybe better than you think. It's not other people you don't trust, Clara. It's yourself."

His dark eyes were warm with understanding and once more she felt something pulling them together, just like it had the night in the barn under the glittering stars.

"Maybe," he whispered, "one day you won't feel the need to hold back so much. Maybe one day you'll trust yourself enough to let someone in."

When had he gotten so close? All she'd have to do was lean forward the slightest bit and she could feel the warmth of him. Another step and she could tilt up her face and touch her lips to his. Just one more…

Rattler got sick of standing still and tossed his head, shaking Ty's arm and making his bridle hardware jingle in the clear, cold air.

"We should mount up," he said, but his voice sounded all husky and soft.

"We should," she murmured, and then threw caution to the north wind, stood on tiptoe and pressed her mouth to his.

She clutched the reins tightly to keep her hands from reaching out to him. The contact of her lips on his was enough. More than enough. The hard wall of his body was against hers and even through the heavy jacket it felt intimate. Just this much. She wanted just this much to hold close to her heart. When he kissed her this way she could temporarily forget all the ways she'd failed. All the mistakes she'd made.

"Drop the reins," he murmured against her mouth. "Please, Clara."

She obeyed, letting the leather dangle to the ground as he also let go of Rattler's.

The next moment she was in his arms. One hand cupped her head, warm against the knitted cap, while the other pressed against the small of her back, pulling her flush against his body as he spread his feet, anchoring the both of them to the hard ground. The kiss lost its sweetness and blossomed into something wild and primitive and beautiful, and she clutched at the shoulder of his coat, a lifeline to keep herself from coming completely unglued.

"Clara," he murmured, sliding his lips along her jaw and touching the hollow just below her earlobe. A delicious shiver ran down her body and she heard herself gasp as he tasted the spot with his tongue. The hand that had been cupping her head moved, grazing her shoulder as it traveled down the front of her coat. Shock rippled through Clara's body. If it weren't for the coat he would know exactly what his touch was doing to her. She swallowed, tried desperately to clear her head. She wasn't ready. Her body was crying out for her to be but she wasn't. She captured his hand in her fingers.

"I can't," she whispered. Even in the brisk breeze, her hushed words were clear as a bell.

He squeezed her hand, but his lips were still busy doing marvellous things to her earlobe and the delicate skin of her neck. "I'll slow down," he suggested, his breath warm and slightly damp and altogether far too arousing.

For the space of a few seconds she gave in, letting out a shaky breath as her head tipped back, allowing him easier access to her throat. But when his arm tightened around her again, pinning their bodies together, she knew they had to stop. Now.

"Please, Ty, please don't do this." She nearly sounded like she was sobbing and she wasn't sure if it was from fear of taking this to the ultimate conclusion or if it was just all too much for her senses to handle.

He loosened his grip, hesitated, then pressed one last heartbreakingly sweet kiss on the sensitive side of her chin. "You're killing me, Clara."

"I didn't mean to. I just wanted to kiss you."

Oh, good Lord. She sounded about thirteen and just as green.

"Mission accomplished." She felt his lips curve against her cheek. "God, woman. What am I going to do with you?"

She relaxed, knowing he'd finally heeded her plea and he wasn't angry. "I don't know. I like you, Ty. I care for you. But I'm not sure I'll ever be able to give anyone anything more. I'm sorry I misled you. You're probably used to women who are more confident."

She couldn't make herself look him in the eye.

"I'm not mad. Frustrated? Maybe." His voice was rich and seductive. "But you didn't mislead me, Clara. Not ever. And I wouldn't want you to change one hair on your head. You're worth far more than any of those other girls."

Her cheeks felt hot, even in the wintery air. "You don't have to say that."

He tilted her chin up so she was forced to look at him. There was no teasing on his face. And he wasn't just being polite. He was absolutely sincere. "I said it and I meant it. I shouldn't have pushed. I got caught up." The corner of his mouth turned up in a boyish smile. "That's what you do to me. You make me forget all my good intentions."

She sighed, but then caught him staring at her lips again. "You'd better mount up," he warned softly, "before I change my mind."

She scurried off to grab Herb's reins and with weak knees put her foot in the stirrup.

Ty was the honorable one here. Ty was the solid, stable one who despite popular opinion really did seem to always do the right thing.

This couldn't happen again. No more time alone. No more sneaking away just the two of them. It was too tempting. Because it wasn't Ty who'd run scared when it was all over. It was her.

She had fallen under his spell, but this wasn't what she wanted. There was no future for them. There was only her future. She'd never let anyone have the power to hurt her again. She'd never again let anyone break her heart again. And Ty was just the sort of man who could do it. He was already doing it.

She didn't wait for Ty's command. She pointed Herb in the direction of the ranch and started for home. It was time she stuck to doing her job and locked her personal feelings away. Because Ty, without even trying, made her forget all the important lessons she'd learned.

The snow held off overnight, but by the time Clara arrived at Diamondback the next morning, the first hard, flinty flakes were starting to fall, promising a miserable day ahead. The kitchen, however, was bright and warm and welcoming; Molly had a pot of coffee perking and the air still smelled of bacon and pancakes and maple syrup. The scent of it was homey and sweet.

This was exactly the sort of thing she couldn't get used to. She had to remember that this wasn't her home, and this wasn't her family. Ty was right. She did hold people at arm's length, refusing to let them too close. There were reasons for that. You let people in and soon they discovered your vulnerabilities. And then they found ways to exploit them. Jackson had been a champ at it. He'd used his innate charm—the man he showed the world to win her over time and time again. To give her hope. She'd hoped that telling him about the baby would change things. She'd seen him with his nephews. "Uncle" Jackson had been warm and caring and gentle. Getting pregnant had been unin-

tentional, but she'd deluded herself into thinking Jackson
would change once he knew.

She hadn't expected the jealous rage. The accusations.

She'd stayed awake long into the night last night, thinking about it. There had been two sides to Jackson and
she'd seen them both. She knew Ty was different. But was
she willing to take a chance on being wrong? She'd been
wrong before, after all.

Molly had her hands in a sink full of dishwater as a
troubled Clara hung up her coat and tucked her scarf into
her sleeve, determined to let her dark thoughts go. She
had a job to do.

"Oh, Clara," Molly said. "I nearly called you and told
you to stay home today. I fear the weather's going to turn
nasty."

"It's okay. I can always put Virgil through his paces
and then head back at lunchtime." The prospect of a short
workday suddenly held a certain appeal. The one bright
spot in her evening last night had been arriving home to
find a letter on the table. She'd written to her aunt, who
had gotten in touch with Clara's mom, and now her mom
had replied with a letter and an open invitation to visit her
new condo anytime.

Clara wasn't sure what would happen next or when, but
they'd made contact. It was an exciting first step. Maybe
if she went home after lunch she could write a response,
or even call the number her mom had written on the bot-
tom of the letter.

"There's lots of room here if the roads get bad." Molly
smiled and wiped her hands on a dishcloth. "You know
how he perks up when you're around. You're good for
him."

Clara assumed Molly was talking about Virgil and not
Tyson, but a warmth spread through her just the same at

the compliment. What was it about Diamondback that felt like coming home? Yet it did. This house—that she only visited—felt more like home than her own room with her belongings did at Butterfly House. Yet another feeling Clara knew she shouldn't get used to.

Molly's face fell, though, as she reached for a tray that still contained a plate of uneaten breakfast. "Virgil barely touched his breakfast, even though I made bacon and buckwheat pancakes, his favorite."

Clara frowned, shifting her brain into work mode. Virgil always ate a hearty morning meal. To not eat—especially his favorites—was definitely out of character. "Did he take his meds okay?"

Molly nodded. "Yes, with his juice. He said he was tired so I left him to nap, oh, maybe an hour ago?"

Clara forced a smile. The heavy, persistent feeling she'd had lately came back, sending tingles down her spine. Ever since the day Ty had spoken to his father, Virgil had been quiet. He'd done his exercises but without the ornery, determined edge Clara was used to. He hadn't been eating as well, either, picking at the meals Molly made him. Clara had chalked it up to not being as hungry. Now that the weather was turning cold, Virgil spent less time outside, and she'd thought maybe his appetite was adjusting according to his activity level.

But for him to barely touch a favorite? Clara thought back over the last weeks. She compared that man to the one who had been so insistent that he'd walk Angela down the aisle.

Virgil had been failing. She hadn't done her job, had she? She'd seen the signs but hadn't wanted to believe it. She'd taken his vitals and put him through his paces but she'd ignored the other obvious tells because she'd wanted to believe he was getting better. She'd put it down to simple aging. What if it was something more?

"I'll tiptoe in and check on him," Clara suggested. And if he was awake, she was going to give him a stern talking-to and let him know that from now on she was going to be dogging his heels big time. No more meals in his room. She was going to have him up and about and at the dining table three times a day.

She made her way to the bedroom, her footsteps slowing as she walked on the soft hallway carpet. Virgil had a doctor's appointment in a few weeks, but perhaps it was time to call and move it up. To make sure there wasn't something going on that they didn't know about.

The door was open a crack and she pushed it gently so she could peer in. Virgil's eyes were closed, his face peaceful. Clara's eyes burned. She'd seen that look before. Too peaceful.

She went inside, felt for a pulse, bit down on her lip. Swallowed around the lump in her throat. All the resolutions she'd made during the walk down the hall evaporated. It was too late.

For a long moment she stood there, unsure of what to do next. It didn't seem possible that he could be gone—just like that. Molly was going to be so devastated, and Ty and Sam...

The air seemed to burn a path into her lungs as she gasped for breath. Poor Molly. Finally Clara moved into action. She straightened the blankets, tucking them neatly around his chest. Tenderly brushed his hair with her fingertips until it lay flat and smooth. When Molly came in, Clara wanted her to see a loving husband who had simply gone to sleep. It was a moment Molly would always remember. Clara couldn't take away the pain but she could do this one thing to perhaps make the memory easier.

A barrage of emotions threatened to break free, but Clara held them in, knowing she had too much to do right now to fall apart. This family had given her a second chance. Maybe Ty had been right. Maybe she did hold herself away from them all. And she'd just resolved to distance herself even more.

Those thoughts evaporated in the face of Virgil's death. She would be there for them. Help them through this as best she could. As Virgil's nurse. But more than that—as a friend. They deserved more, but she could give them that much.

She laid her hand on the blanket one last time. "I am going to miss you," she whispered, and sniffled. The tears she hadn't wanted to shed slid free and burned their way down her cheeks. It didn't matter what she said or how she rationalized anything. She *loved* this family.

She should have done more. She shouldn't have let herself get so personally involved that she wore rose-colored glasses where Virgil was concerned. She'd failed him, hadn't she? And so she'd failed them all by letting her feelings blind her to what was happening before her eyes.

She swiped the tears away with the back of her hand, determined to pull herself together. She would miss him. His garrulous teasing, the way he winked at her, even the way he grumbled during physio. She'd miss the way his eyes lit up when Molly came in the room. What would it be like to have that sort of love? It made her heart hurt just thinking about it.

Then she took a breath, squared her shoulders and set about the terrible job of telling Molly the news.

CHAPTER EIGHT

THE CHURCH WAS PACKED with mourners, the overflow parking a line of cars and heavy-duty half-ton trucks along the shoulder of the road. Angela had kindly offered Clara a seat with her and Sam, but Clara had refused. Today was for family. She sat, instead, about halfway back and by herself.

The snow that had held off for so long had arrived in earnest the night after Virgil's death. Outside, the prairie was pristine and white. Every time the church door opened, a gust of frigid air blustered its way in; it was cold on her legs and she tucked them farther beneath the pew. Her black skirt and sweater provided little warmth against the subzero temperatures, so she hugged her arms around herself, waiting for the family to be seated and the service to start.

When the minister escorted the family in, Clara's hand flew to her mouth in alarm. Tyson looked terrible, as though he hadn't slept for days. He was clean-shaven and once more in the dark suit he'd worn to Sam's wedding just a few months earlier. But the careless disorder of his hair was now severely tamed, and he had bags beneath his eyes.

Her heart broke for all of them, but particularly for Ty. He'd just gotten his father back only to lose him once more—and forever. She watched as he sat between Molly and Sam, and she stared at the breadth of his shoulders. They looked somehow narrower now that he was hunched over slightly. Molly leaned over and whispered something in his ear and he nodded and attempted a smile.

But Clara knew what Ty's smile looked like, and that wasn't it. Everything she knew—and loved—about him was buried beneath his grief, and her heart broke for him.

The service itself was lovely, a true testament to the pillar of the community that Virgil had been over the years. Sam delivered a heartfelt, emotional eulogy that had Clara, and several others, wiping their eyes. But it was when he mentioned Ty's return that Ty's head snapped up and he met his brother's gaze. "Only one thing meant more to my dad than Diamondback," Sam said. "And that was his family. He was so happy that Ty had come home. That his boys were going to be working Diamondback together, the way it was meant to be. Dad, your life wasn't quite finished, but I know your heart is at rest, because the family is back together again."

Sam paused, collected himself and carried on. But Clara saw Angela slide over on the pew next to Ty and put her arm around his shoulders. Clara reached inside her purse for a tissue and wiped her eyes and nose. This had to be killing him. And she suddenly regretted not accepting the invitation to sit with the family. This went beyond her own fears and resolutions. Ty was a friend. She should have put her own issues aside for today and been there for him.

When it was over, the family exited first. Ty's eyes were red, and for a fraction of a second his gaze caught hers before he looked away. The pain in his eyes cut into her with the sharpness of a knife blade. Virgil was gone. None of them would ever hear his rusty laugh or see his

smile and twinkling eyes again. He had been more than a
client. It had been more than a job. She might as well stop
pretending otherwise. For all her trying to keep the Diamonds at arm's length, they'd managed—all of them—to
sneak past her defenses. Especially Ty.

He would always hold a piece of her heart, even as she
prepared to leave Cadence Creek forever. There was no
real reason to stay now, was there? She no longer had a
job. And she had her own family waiting.

Angela touched her arm in the vestibule. "There's a
reception back at the house. The church ladies have put
together sandwiches and sweets and coffee. You should
come, Clara."

"I will," she answered.

Angela's face blanked with surprise. "That easily? You
were so hesitant earlier."

"I was wrong." She squeezed Angela's fingers. "Ty's
a wreck, isn't he?"

"He was fine for a while. You remember. He rolled up
his sleeves and did what needed to be done."

Clara did remember. After she'd broken the news to
Molly, Molly had called Sam and Ty. Sam had cried but
Ty had remained dry-eyed, holding everyone together.
While Sam and Angela and Molly talked about arrange-
ments, Ty had done the practical thing and looked after
the stock and chores. Clara had asked what she could do
but there was nothing. In an effort to do something help-
ful, she'd spent a few hours putting together some food
while the family followed the ambulance to the hospital
and from there to the funeral home.

But she had gone home to Butterfly House before they
returned rather than feel like an intruder, arriving home
ahead of the snowstorm.

She'd told Ty to call if he needed anything.

He hadn't called.

"But?" she asked Angela. She knew there was a *but* coming.

"But yesterday it became clear he wasn't sleeping. He's running on autopilot and I'm not sure how much longer he can keep it up. I know you're not involved, you know, romantically, but he needs a friend."

Not involved? Clara blinked. She was in it up to her eyeballs. Ty hadn't slept but she hadn't either for worrying and wondering how he was coping. And then the invitation from her mom had come and more decisions were up for grabs. The tossing and turning was getting to her, too.

This was the last thing she could do for Ty before she had to say goodbye, she supposed. Someone needed to be there for him rather than the other way around.

"I'll get my coat and meet you there," she assured Angela.

The house was already crammed with people when she arrived. She had to park along the side of the driveway, a long way away from the house, and she made her way carefully along the ploughed surface in her heels. When she got to the porch, she saw Buster tied outside. He was lying in a back corner of the verandah, his nose between his paws, and his eyes were the sorriest eyes she'd ever seen on a dog. He'd lost his master and he'd been evicted from his warm bed. She took a moment and went to him, squatting down and resting her weight on her high heels as she stroked his fur.

"Hey, boy," she crooned, rubbing the silky crown of his head. "Lost your place today, huh? If it weren't so cold, I think I'd rather stay out here with you in the quiet. All those people…hmmm."

He lifted his head, and when she stopped patting he nudged her palm. She laughed lightly.

"Feels good, doesn't it?" She patted his neck. "Don't worry, Buster. It's only temporary."

"It's nicer out here, isn't it?"

The deep timbre of his voice surprised her, and a shiver of pleasure rippled up her body before she could even think about it. "Ty."

She looked over her shoulder. Goodness, he looked even more terrible up close. Haunted, she realized. She pushed up from the squat and brushed her hands down her skirt, unsure of what to say next. I'm sorry? She'd already said that days ago.

"I'm glad you came," he said quietly, taking a step forward.

"Of course I did." And then she did what she'd wanted to do since first seeing him at the church: she went to him and wrapped her arms around him.

He didn't hug back right away, but after a few seconds his arms tightened around her middle and held her close. "I needed this," he murmured in her ear. "Thank you."

"Anytime," she said back, but knew she was a liar. She wouldn't be here long enough to make that true.

He let her go and stepped back. "You must be freezing. Let's go inside. I could do with a cup of coffee."

Inside the house was loud—how could it be otherwise with so many people crowding up the living room and kitchen? The dining table had been extended with every leaf and was laden with platters of sandwiches and squares. A catering-size coffee urn was on the butcher block next to a stack of foam cups and wooden stir sticks. Everywhere around her, voices expressed sympathy and shared stories of Virgil's life. Molly was in the middle, smiling and holding a paper plate with a few sandwiches and sweets. But Clara noticed she wasn't eating them. Not a single bite was taken from the triangles of bread with some unnamed filling inside.

Ty held a cup of coffee in his hands but nothing else. "When did you eat last?" she asked him, pouring herself a cup of tea. She took a sip and blinked. It was strong enough to dance the Hornpipe on, so she added extra milk and hoped for the best.

"I'm fine," he replied, nodding at a passing neighbor who was on his way to the door.

"You're not fine." She stood in front of him so his body afforded her a bit of privacy from the eyes of the room. "You're tired and gaunt and not eating properly. Let me fix you a plate."

"You're not going to let it go, are you?"

"No."

"Fine. I'll eat something."

She went to the table and selected what looked like roast beef and minced ham sandwiches, leaving the pretty but insubstantial offerings like cream cheese and cherry to more delicate tastes. Beside that she added sliced pickles and several pieces of cheese, a brownie and what looked like something lemony with a coconut topping. When she presented it to him he raised an eyebrow. "I went for the most manly items I could," she said.

"How long do these things usually last?"

She shrugged. "Hopefully not long. You all look exhausted."

"I'm fine."

She picked up a sandwich from his plate and bit into it, hoping a little competition would get his appetite going. "So you said." Her tone definitely let him know that she didn't believe a word of it.

Molly approached and put her hand on Ty's arm. "Oh, good, you're eating."

Clara gave him a telling look and he scowled back at her.

"Thank you for coming, Clara. I'm afraid we seemed a bit lost without you here the last few days. It's good to see Ty actually eat something rather than promise to and then hardly nibble."

Molly's words made her feel even worse for staying away. "Oh, Molly, I wish you'd called. I would have come. I didn't want to intrude on family time. If there's anything you need…"

But again there was a bittersweet edge to her words. She meant them and yet she knew that her time was limited. It was simply a platitude and she hated that she'd done that. She'd been on the receiving end of too many over the years.

"We're fine," Molly said. "It'll get easier. I have my boys here and Angela and I hope you'll come to see us even though…"

Molly's eyes suddenly misted with tears. "Oh, dear."

Even though Clara no longer had a job. No one really had to say it, did they?

And so Clara spoke from the heart when she said the next words. "You were always more than an employer to me, Molly, you know that."

"The wedding ring quilt still needs finishing. One last roll before I bind it off. You're welcome to pick up a needle and thread anytime."

Clara's heart seized, thinking of the lovely times she and Molly had shared stitching the beautiful wedding ring pattern. She wished she could be here and for a moment almost reconsidered. But it wasn't practical. She had a home waiting in Moose Jaw and a job to look for and she couldn't remain at Butterfly House forever.

Instead of replying she did something she hadn't done

before—she hugged Molly. A genuine, squeezy, heart-felt hug.

Molly hugged back.

They pulled apart and sniffed a little. "I'd better keep moving," Molly said. "So many people."

Clara turned back to Ty but he was gone. She saw him across the room talking to one of the ranch hands who had put on his best jeans and starched shirt for the somber occasion. Was it just her or had the lines around Ty's eyes eased just a little bit? Why hadn't someone made sure he was taking care of himself?

Then again, it wasn't her job, was it?

After another hour, the church ladies packed up their tins and Tupperware and coffee pots. Clara helped move leftover sandwiches to a platter for the fridge—an easy meal for the family later. The stragglers made their way until it was just Sam, Angela, Molly, Ty and Clara left standing in the silence.

"I suppose I should pick up the things from Mr. Burgess," Molly said, referring to the funeral director. She let out a long sigh.

"Let us do that," Sam suggested. "You've had enough, don't you think?"

"I'm fine."

Clara stepped forward. "I've heard that from someone else today, too. A good gust of wind would topple you right over. You're exhausted. Let us look after you."

The lack of a reply told Clara all she needed to know.

She looked at Sam. "I'll stay. You and Angela look after what you need to. I'll putter around here and make sure Molly takes it easy."

"You're a gem," Sam replied, dropping a kiss on her cheek. She found she didn't even mind. When he straightened he took Angela's hand in his. Clara had noticed them holding hands a lot today. They had each other, loved each other, were there for each other. What did it feel like to love someone and feel so utterly secure that you could trust them with everything?

Ty nodded at his brother. "I'll help Clara and look after the stock."

"Sounds good." Sam gave his mother a kiss and pointed a finger at her. "Do what Clara says, and let us handle the rest for today."

Clara shooed Molly to bed after Sam and Angela were gone, and returned shortly after with a small tea tray holding a cup of hot cocoa and two warm scones topped with Molly's favorite jam. "Your favorites," she announced softly, stepping inside the bedroom. She'd only been in this room once before—Molly had always stayed in the downstairs room with Virgil after his stroke. But this had been the master bedroom, and Molly looked tiny and fragile in the middle of the king-size bed.

"What would I do without you, Clara?"

She sat down on the edge of the bed. "I'm sorry I wasn't here the past few days. I didn't want to get in the way."

"I thought Ty would have called you. Or perhaps this was too hard for you for some reason."

"Ty doesn't like to ask for help," Clara pointed out. "Anyway, I'm here now. And I'm going to make you promise to drink every sip and eat every bite and then have a nap."

"Yes, ma'am." Molly held up the cup and took a drink of the rich cocoa.

"Right. I'll come back for the tray in a bit."

She was at the door when Molly's voice called her back. "Clara?"

She paused, her hand on the door. "Hmm?"

Molly's voice thickened. "Virgil loved you, you know.

We used to talk about it alone. We understood you'd had a terrible time, but I think he had a secret hope that you and Ty might…well, you're good for our son. He's a different man since he came home."

Nothing Molly might have said could have cut any deeper. Ty had kissed her and there was definitely something between them, but he'd never even breathed a word about anything more permanent. And what if he did? Clara was smart enough to know that she'd probably go running for the hills. A woman could only take so many disappointments, after all. Maybe Ty was a different man but she still doubted she was the woman for him. He was the rodeo star with the belt buckles and a wagonload of experience. She'd only ever been with one man, and it had been enough for a lifetime.

"If Ty is different, it's all down to him," Clara replied. "Maybe he grew up. It takes some people longer than others."

She shut the door with a quiet click and leaned against it. And sometimes people just stayed stuck, didn't they? Like her. Would she ever have a normal life where none of this mattered anymore?

Ty couldn't bear the thought of going back to the house.

The chores were done and the watery afternoon light had dimmed to a thin twilight, casting gray shadows over the snow. He stood in the barn doorway and saw the lights glowing warmly from the kitchen windows; looked farther up the length of the driveway and saw Clara's car still sitting halfway to the road, a bump on the otherwise lonely stretch of gravel. She was still here. And he was too raw to face her right now. To face anyone.

Today had been about saying goodbye, but he hadn't been able to. Not at the funeral, surrounded by all those people. Not sitting next to Molly, who was counting on him to hold it together, or next to Sam, who'd been the apple of Virgil's eye for over thirty years. He'd had nowhere to put his grief and instead it had built and built until he stood here in the barn and thought he might explode with it all.

Even the physical exertion of mucking out stalls hadn't been enough of a displacement activity.

He fisted his hands, pressing them against the massive door frame. He should have come home sooner. He should have made amends sooner. Should, should, should. All the things he'd put off, all the mistakes he'd made. Regret tasted bitter in his mouth. If he'd been here all along, he could have spared Virgil some of the heavy load of running Diamondback.

Now it was too late. And the man he'd loved and respected and even at times despised for pushing him so hard was gone.

The breath left Ty's chest as the grief finally struck, hard and sharp and with the jarring thud of hitting the dirt after being bucked off. For a moment he stood, paralyzed with it until he heard the first harsh sob escape his mouth. The sound was so foreign, so unfamiliar that it frightened him. It was followed by another, and another.

He had to get out of the doorway. He stumbled down the corridor, past the stalls to the storeroom and his office. Once inside he sat on the edge of the fold-out army cot Sam had kept there for long nights during animal births or illnesses. He put his head in his hands and let it come, finally—all the pain and hurt and self-loathing and other myriad emotions he couldn't even name but that had threatened to overwhelm him for days.

He'd loved his father—and Virgil had been his father in all the ways that truly mattered.

His biggest regret was that he'd never been man enough
to say the words. And Virgil had died not knowing.

When Ty didn't come back from the barn, Clara started
to get worried. Molly was sound asleep and there wasn't
a speck of dirt to be found in the kitchen. She looked out
the deck doors towards the barn. The lights were off—all
except for one tiny glow from the room she now knew Ty
used as an office.

She put on her coat and borrowed a pair of Molly's
boots, slipping out the door and heading towards the long,
low structure.

Inside was quiet and dark, until she heard a low, muffled sound. Her stomach knotted as she followed the noise,
down the corridor with her boots making soft steps on the
concrete. The door to the office was open a few inches,
and peering inside, she saw him—sitting on the army cot
and weeping.

For the space of a breath she considered tiptoeing back
out and leaving him to his grief privately, but in the end
she couldn't make herself walk away. She pushed the door
open, went to his side and put her hand on his shoulder.

"Tyson," she whispered.

His head snapped up, his face a terrible mixture of
pain, surprise and embarrassment. "It's okay," she murmured, squeezing the wide shoulder beneath her fingers.
"Let it out."

His arms looped around her hips, drawing her close,
and she felt his breath through her jacket and hot against
her belly as he pressed his face against her. Touched,
drowned in sympathy and love for him, she rested her
hands on his head, gently stroking his soft hair as he cried.

"He didn't know," Ty said, his breath hitching. "Dammit. I didn't want to fall apart like this."

"What didn't he know?"

Ty shuddered. Clara slid out of his embrace, taking a seat beside him on the cot. She reached over and took his hand. "What didn't he know, Ty?"

"How I felt about him. I couldn't ever say the words. He…he took me in even though doing it meant admitting his own sister was a failure. He stopped being my uncle at that moment and became my father. But I always resented him. I felt sorry for myself. I told myself he loved Sam more than me."

"But he didn't. You know that."

Ty shook his head. "I was such a screwup. I had something to prove and I didn't care who I hurt to do it. Mom, Dad, Sam… I was good at what I did and it was an added bonus to rub their noses in it."

"Ty," she said softly, knowing he had to get out the feelings but also knowing they weren't accurate. "This is the grief talking. You're being too hard on yourself."

"No," he insisted, resting his elbows on his knees. "I was wrong. I knew it long ago but was too proud to admit it and come home where I belonged. It took an invitation from Sam and a request for help. I was so proud that I had to be *needed,* don't you understand? And now he's gone. I gave up the chance to show him what I could do. To show him I've grown up. That I loved and admired him."

"He knew."

Ty shook his head. "How could he possibly know?"

"You're human," she soothed. "You're strong. You're independent. And most of all, you're a good man, Ty. He knew that. Look how he felt about your new plans. Believe me, he gave them his stamp of approval far easier than he gave it to Sam this year. He loved you for exactly who you are. He was proud of you—for your accomplishments, for your successes. Love, Ty…" She swallowed as she folded his hand inside her own. "Love isn't conditional on never making mistakes, or being flawed, or afraid. It just is. So go ahead and grieve for him and miss him. But please, please, don't regret what can't be changed now. You came home and made amends. It was the greatest gift you could have given him."

His face was tear-streaked, his rich brown eyes rimmed with red and his cheeks were chapped from rubbing them. But as Ty lifted his face and gazed into her eyes, she knew she was done for. She loved him. Not for his charm or sexy swagger, but for the heart he kept so closely guarded inside. She loved him for his flaws and insecurities and all the things that made him want to be a better man when he was already pretty darn amazing to begin with.

And because she loved him, it killed her to see him hurting so much. She cupped his face in her hands and leaned in, kissing each of his bruised eyelids as her lip wobbled uncontrollably. Never, never in her life had she felt this raw and exposed with anyone. And while that was terrifying in itself, the truly amazing thing was that it felt *right*.

Her lips lingered on the crest of his cheek as she hesitated. Their breaths mingled as something extraordinary shifted, curling deliciously through her body as they both froze, paused in the prolonged moment, on the edge of something monumental.

She forgot how to breathe.

Then his hand was on the nape of her neck, holding her in place while his mouth clashed with hers, full of passion and pain and acceptance.

There was no fear. No hesitation, no questions, nothing but Ty and the feel of his mouth on hers and the energy flowing between them. Desperately she clung to his shoulders, well aware that they were perfectly alone in the dark with only the pale circle of the desk lamp's glow giving any light in the room and leaving the corners black and hidden. The kiss was edgy and full-on and held nothing back, and it was glorious and devastating and out of control.

With trembling fingers she reached for the buttons of his flannel shirt, needing to make a connection in the midst of her own confusing grief, needing to touch his warm skin. She shoved it off his shoulders and he broke off the kiss, sitting back and searing her with his gaze while he hastily pulled it off his arms and dropped it to the floor. Her heart leapt as his voice came soft and husky in the dimness. "Touch me."

He was warm and smooth beneath her fingertips as she ran her hand down the center of his chest, over the taut skin of his ribs and back up to his shoulder. Her fingertips touched a puckered scar by his rotator cuff and she wondered how he'd got it. His eyes closed and his lips fell open and she marvelled that she could possibly have such an effect on a man like him. Momentarily she paused, daunted by the idea of the experienced women who had come before her. But then Ty opened his eyes and reached for her coat. "I want to see you, too," he said.

She didn't answer as he unzipped her coat and let it fall behind her. She was still in her sweater and skirt and he reached for the hem of the sweater, pulling it up and off with tantalizing slowness.

She sat before him in her bra and felt her face flame. What was she doing? She should get up and leave right now before they got to a point where they couldn't turn back. But her feet felt as though they were made of concrete blocks and she didn't move. Goosebumps erupted over her skin, tiny points of sensation as he pulled her close, and for the first time in two years she was pressed, flesh to flesh, against a man.

It was so different. So warm and alluring and…luxurious. His skin was warm pressed against hers and he kissed her again, longer, slower, with promises of things to come.

Wonderful things, she realized, giving herself over to the sensation. Ty would not hurt her. She trusted him completely. And even though a tiny voice inside her head echoed with a smidgen of common sense—that Ty was acting out of grief, that they both were—she ignored it.

She was lying on the cot now, looking up at him as his tough, lean body pressed her into the mattress. "I need you," he murmured, touching the soft skin at her temple with a finger.

"You have me," she replied, reaching for him.

CHAPTER NINE

SUNLIGHT FILTERED weakly through the office window as Clara turned her head and the full impact of what she'd done slammed into her.

Ty slept, his lashes peaceful against his still-tanned-from-the-summer cheeks. A rough blanket covered them both, but he'd pushed it down on his slice of the army cot so that it bunched around his hips. Even relaxed she could see the curves and dips of the muscles in his chest and arms. He was beautiful. And he'd been...

She stopped the thought before she could finish it. Her cheeks flared with heat. She didn't want to think about how gentle he'd been. How intense. How consuming. She'd been shameless, caught up in the emotion of the day, needing that connection with another human being, needing to be there for him when he was hurting so much.

Making love to Ty had been nothing short of perfect—beautiful, without fear, without agenda or power. It had been giving, not taking. She hadn't known it could be like that. Hadn't known it could make her feel so...full.

And now that it was over, and the sun was coming up, it was scary as hell.

She needed to get out of here before he woke up. He couldn't see her this way. She shivered as the cold air touched her bare skin, raising goosebumps. How could she have forgotten all her rules so easily? Had she really thought she loved him last night?

She looked down at him one last time, tenderness washing over her. She *did* love him. In a way she hadn't known she could love. It threatened to swallow her up with its hugeness. What about her plans? She'd let her feelings for someone derail her before, hadn't she? And that had ended in the worst sort of disaster. It had taken everything from her. The one thing she'd been sure of since the day she walked away was that she was going to be completely self-sufficient. How could she do that if she kept getting swept up in Tyson?

And then there was her family. She wanted to get them back again. To reconnect. How could she turn her back on her mom's invitation to stay with her? To set back the clock and start again?

Clara slipped out from beneath the blanket and off the army cot as Ty took a deep breath and exhaled. She froze, hoping his eyes would remain closed. When he stilled once more, she reached for her panties and bra and slipped them on, followed quickly by her skirt and sweater. She kept her gaze on his face as she stuffed her pantyhose into a ball and shoved her feet into Molly's boots. Last night was supposed to be nothing more than a hug and a healthy dose of empathy. A kind ear to listen as he talked it out.

But there'd been little talking. From the moment she'd found him, the simple hug of sympathy had blazed into a passionate fire that quickly burned out of control the moment he'd touched his lips to hers.

On tiptoe she crept out of the tack room. Right now she had to get back to the house and from there, home. He wouldn't follow her to Butterfly House, she knew that. She'd be safe there. With a pain in her heart she realized she wouldn't be back. There was no need for her now. Her job was over. It was all over.

She was nearly to the door when his voice stopped her. "Clara."

It wasn't a question. It wasn't quite a command. But it stopped her in her tracks and made her bite down on her lip. She didn't turn around, but folded her arms over her chest as a blast of cold air came through the open barn door.

"You're running away?"

He had come up behind her, close enough she could feel the heat radiating off his body and smell the warm, male scent of him. She trembled, so incredibly tempted to turn and find shelter in his arms again. But she had to be stronger than that. Ty wasn't for her. They both knew it. And yet there was an edge of hurt in his question that snuck past all her resolve and hit its mark.

"I didn't want to wake you."

It sounded weak even to her ears, and he hadn't bought it either as he huffed out a bitter laugh. "Right. Well, I deserve that. I mean usually I'm the one sneaking out, right? Ty Diamond the player, isn't that what you said before? What am I now? Your dirty little secret? After all, I doubt too many residents of Butterfly House do the walk of shame that often."

If he was trying to sound flippant he was failing miserably. He flayed her with his words, each one a little stinging whip of insult. There was such bitterness in them, such pain. She remembered the words she'd nearly said to him last night and felt relieved she hadn't said them out loud. At least she wouldn't regret *that*.

She didn't know what to say and seconds ticked by. Why couldn't he just turn around and go back in the barn? Let her go? She should be the one to walk away. This was his home. And yet the pain in her chest persisted. Last night had been the first time she'd been intimate with a man since walking away from Jackson. It was the first time she'd *enjoyed* it in longer than she could remember. Ty had made that possible. He would always be special because of it. No matter what he said now, she wouldn't let him take that away. She hadn't frozen, like Jackson had so often accused her of doing. She'd let herself feel every sensation and emotion and it had been heavenly.

"I'm sorry," she whispered, turning around.

It wasn't the right thing to say. His face that had been so relaxed and beautiful in sleep had a hard edge now, a mask to hide any sort of emotion. She'd seen that look more than once over the past weeks when he'd crossed swords with his father. It was his brittle protective layer. Lately it had been gone, and she hated that she was the one to put it back. She should have known better last night. She should have walked away and let him grieve in peace.

He shrugged as if her apology meant nothing. "I just thought you might want this so no one else found it and asked questions."

He dangled an earring from his fingers. The smile on his lips wasn't tender, but hard-edged and mocking. But there was something in his eyes—a flicker—that sent a spiral of guilt curling through her. She'd hurt him. She'd only wanted to help and instead she'd made it worse.

They'd made it worse.

She took the earring from his fingers. "It's not like that, Ty. I'm not ashamed."

He shrugged again, making the muscles in his shoulders flex, as though it didn't matter if she was or wasn't. He'd slipped his shirt on but left it unbuttoned, revealing an alluring slice of chest. Was it any wonder she'd fallen under his spell? He was the most beautiful specimen of manhood she'd ever seen, hard and honed from years of hard work and rodeo. He had his share of scars but he'd healed and come back for more.

As if he was punishing himself.

"It's exactly like that, Clara. There's no sense in pretending it's not."

Panic started to grip her. Realizing she'd abandoned her rules was one thing. Doing an analysis after the fact was terrifying. She was torn between needing to escape and needing him to understand. He had taken something that had made her so afraid and made it beautiful, relaxed and liberating. But to explain meant she'd have to admit that she had feelings. She couldn't have made love to him otherwise.

"Secret, yes," she admitted, forcing herself to stare directly into his eyes. "But not dirty. I would prefer to keep this private, Ty. It's no one else's business and it's not going to happen again."

"You're sure about that?"

She swallowed. "Aren't you? I'm not a girl. I know what last night was. It was grief and emotion and needing someone. I'm…I'm glad I was there for you. We were there for each other—I've got my share of grief, too, you know. And a few of my own regrets. You don't hold the corner on that."

"Two ships in the night, is that it? Solace in a time of grief?"

"Wasn't it?" she challenged.

He didn't answer, but she saw doubt cloud his face and wished things could magically be less complicated between them. Wished that they might have met under different circumstances. What if he'd never left home and had run the ranch with Sam, and what if she'd never made such a horrible mess of her life?

You have to play the cards you're dealt, she told herself, lifting her chin.

"I don't for one second think that you love me, Ty. I think you needed me last night, but this is this morning. It's different now. Besides, I'm no longer needed here now that…" Her throat tightened. "Now that Virgil is gone."

"Who says you're not needed?"

Oh, he was going to make this difficult. Why couldn't he have slept on so she could have made her escape? "I was his nurse. What job is there here for me now? Please believe me, Ty. Keeping this between us has nothing to do with being ashamed of what happened. You have a far lower opinion of yourself than anyone else does. And I can't fix that, Ty. Only you can do that."

Oh, wasn't that rich. She was the last person who should be offering advice about self-confidence and worth.

"And yet you're still running away." He shoved his hands in his pockets and she stared at the space where his shirt wrinkled over his wrists. An image flashed through her mind, a picture so vivid and erotic her whole body heated.

An image so intoxicating she knew she wanted it again. Her gaze traveled up to his face once more and now the smile was knowing. He knew exactly where her mind had gone, didn't he?

She couldn't want him again. This couldn't happen again. Because again would lead into what? An affair? A relationship?

Ty Diamond didn't do relationships. Neither did Clara. And an affair with Ty would end in someone getting hurt—specifically, her.

"I've been in contact with my mom," she said quietly. "She's offered me a place to stay and help finding another job. I'm going back to Saskatchewan in a few days. It's time I made up with my own family, don't you think?"

She began to back away. "Just let me go, Ty. Let's leave last night as a nice memory. You're not in the market for anything more than that, and neither am I."

Before either of them could say another word, she ran through the snow to the house.

And she never looked back.

The last place Ty wanted to be was at Butterfly House, surrounded by its residents, Sam, Angela, Molly and of course Clara.

The rambling yellow house was the sort of big, cozy place that welcomed large families, a lot of noise, and generally had a swing set in the back. The kind of place he'd envisioned as damn near perfect growing up, the sort of place you saw on television movies and sitcoms.

The kind of place he'd pictured when he'd thought about what it would have been like to grow up with his real mother and father—if things had been different. Not that Virgil and Molly hadn't been wonderful parents. But as a kid there had always been that knowledge, that bit of sting of the unknown. What it might have been like to know his birth parents. Wondering why it had been so easy for them to hand him off. He couldn't imagine doing that to his own kid. Not that it had ever been an issue. He'd never wanted the wife and kid and white picket fence that everyone seemed to think was necessary.

But there was no swing set in the yard or children laughing here. Instead of growing families, Butterfly House sheltered healing souls. And he'd been unable to resist his sister-in-law when she'd said with shining eyes that her very first resident was preparing to leave, just the way the program was intended. Angela was happy and proud that Clara was beginning a new phase in her life. To mark the occasion, they were having a potluck dinner as a send-off.

He climbed the porch steps carrying a bachelor's offering to such an event: a paper bag of fresh rolls from the bakery. The door opened and the sound of women's laughter bubbled out, making his heart clench.

He was supposed to be celebrating Clara walking out of his life today. He was supposed to be sending her off with a smile and a good-luck wish. Not a single soul knew that they'd spent the night together. Not one person knew how he regretted the sharp words he'd flung at her when she'd tried to sneak out of the barn.

That had hurt. He hadn't known how much a woman walking away *could* hurt until the right woman did it. And instead of being honest about his feelings, he'd lashed out. He sighed. He'd always been the guy with all the right words and moves. Why did those things never work with Clara?

"Ty! You came!"

Angela greeted him at the door, and he pasted on a smile. "Of course I did."

He stepped inside and held on to the paper bag. He heard Clara's sparkling laugh and something twisted inside his gut. He needed to apologize. And he needed to let her go. Over the past forty-eight hours that had become crystal clear. He didn't want her to ever live with the same regrets he had. She needed to be with her family and make things right.

The party was taking place in the large kitchen. The oversized dining table was set for nine, one side squeezing in four spaces so everyone could fit. The island in the middle of the room was already filling with food—salads were laid out and a cake waited in a domed plastic container. A Crock-Pot bubbled with something delicious-smelling, and as Ty put his bag down on the countertop Molly reached inside the oven and took out an enormous chicken-and-broccoli casserole.

Clara came from the pantry and stopped suddenly at the sight of him there. He was gratified when the color rose in her cheeks.

"Clara."

"Tyson," she said quietly.

He forced a smile for the second time in five minutes. "Big day for you. Congratulations."

She swallowed. Conversations flowed all around them, providing a protective bubble as they spoke. "This isn't quite the way I envisioned it happening," she replied. For a moment her eyes deepened with some sort of emotion he didn't want to try to decipher.

"A new start. You're obviously very happy about it. And Angela is thrilled with the first success of her program."

She finally smiled. "There is that. This program was supposed to help me get back on my feet. It's certainly done that."

Silence fell between them, a lull in conversation where he didn't know what more to say, especially with a potential audience.

"But—" Her sad eyes met his again. "I'd trade it for having Virgil back. How are you?"

For a moment anger flared. How dare she ask in that polite tone, as if something bigger hadn't happened between them? Maybe she could pretend that it had meant nothing, but he couldn't. Yes, he'd been overwhelmed. With grief and fatigue and needing, somehow, to feel connected to another human being.

But not just anyone. To Clara. The kind of woman who'd always scared the living hell out of him.

"I'm fine," he replied sharply, and felt like a heel when her face fell. Damn. They'd spent weeks getting to know each other, learning to relax and trust each other. And now he was right back to wondering what to say and do.

Angela and Sam stood by the head of the table and called for everyone's attention, saving Ty—and Clara—from trying to come up with further empty platitudes. He moved to stand beside Molly, taking the time to look at each of the women present. They were all here for the same reason—because they were building a new life for themselves after escaping abusive relationships. A few were relaxed and smiling, listening to Angela speak. One held back from the others, just a bit, trying to stay under the radar. He ran a finger over his lip. She was a wallflower, much in the way Clara had been when they first met. Uncertain and shy. That first night she'd run away from him after the tiniest kiss on her temple. He hadn't known how to deal with her that night.

And now he knew what it was to make love to her. To hold her heart in his hands. He knew the kind of soul she had inside and the hurts that had shaped her life. She had achieved so much whether she realized it or not. She had a bright future ahead of her, with so much more than he had to offer.

She wanted independence and options.

He was locked into Diamondback and he wouldn't have it any other way. It was where he belonged.

The kindest thing was to let her go, wasn't it? To let her have the life she'd worked so hard for?

After the meal Clara was shooed from the kitchen, absolved of kitchen duties on this, her last night in Cadence Creek. He heard Molly talking with a couple of the ladies about starting a weekly craft night, and Sam and

Angela were chatting with the new director about foundation business.

Ty looked at Clara, who was putting her teacup in the dishwasher. "Walk with me?" he asked.

"I guess that would be okay," she answered. "For a minute."

He held the door for her as they stepped onto the front porch. Somehow he had to make things right in the next few minutes. He had to come up with a way to let her go and wish her well. It was the right thing to do. And after years of making mistakes, Ty knew it was time he started doing the right thing instead of the easy thing.

Clara pulled on her mittens as she led the way down the steps and onto the walkway. Dinner had been excruciating, having to smile all the time like she hadn't a care in the world. Truth was, everything was about to change— again. And the ugly truth was she should be more excited about reconnecting with her family and starting over.

But she wasn't. Because there was still a hole in her heart that was distinctly Ty-shaped. And now he'd asked her outside for what she could only assume was a private goodbye.

His boots sounded on the concrete blocks leading to the driveway, and her pulse did the odd patter that it often did simply when he was near. Despite the cold that was a permanent thing now that snow had finally arrived, Clara felt overly warm in her coat. Another consequence of being near Ty. She wished he hadn't asked. Wished he'd just said his goodbye at the door and gone. It would have been easier than *this*.

She stopped next to the farm truck, knowing it hid them from view of the house and also knowing that if she stopped here he'd be able to get in and drive home once they'd said what they needed to say. Briefly she thought of his car, remembering the night he'd taken her to the diner and brought her home afterward. Sitting in the dark that night she'd wondered if he'd kiss her. Standing in the dark now, with just the streetlamp lighting the street, she wondered the same thing. And just like then, she was torn between wanting him to and scared to death he actually might.

He'd put his hat on his head, the dark brim shadowing his face as he shoved his hands into his coat pockets. Clara swallowed, knowing she'd always remember him this way: tall, sexy and with a dangerous edge. The problem was she knew what was behind the edge, and it made it so very difficult to say goodbye.

"Thank you for coming tonight."

He nodded. "You're heading out in the morning?"

"Yes." She clenched her fingers inside the fleece pocket lining. "It'll take me most of the day to get there."

There was silence, then the far-off sound of a train to the northwest. Clara couldn't stand it any longer. One of them had to say something about it. Clear the air so they could leave it behind. "Ty, I'm sorry about the other day. About running off like I did."

She looked up at him but couldn't tell what he was thinking. The angle of the streetlamp's light and his hat made it impossible to see his eyes. He hunched his shoulders and then straightened them again.

"I said some things I shouldn't have, too. I didn't want it to go that way."

"Then why did it?"

Even though she couldn't see his eyes, his gaze seemed to bore into the very center of her. "Because you were running away. I know I'm not the kind of man for you. I know us being together would be a mistake. But you were running like you were ashamed and I was mad on top of everything else."

Ashamed? That was what he thought? It had been fear, pure and simple. She'd worked too hard to find herself again only to lose herself in another relationship. She didn't trust herself. He'd been right about that. And throwing love into the mix made it ten times worse. How could she possibly tell him that, now that he'd said straight up that anything between them was a mistake?

She couldn't, so she looked at her feet and said, "I wanted to get out of there before anyone would notice my car in the driveway."

The harsh, dry laugh was bitter and she saw his boots turn away. He walked a few feet before turning back. "Clara Ferguson," he said clearly. "You are a lot of things, but I never, ever took you for a coward."

Frustration simmered. Why did he have to make this so hard? He should just let her go, right? What was one night to a man like Ty? He'd broken hearts before, she was sure of it. Had each one been entitled to this touching goodbye? The sarcastic words sat on her tongue. The only thing keeping her from blurting them out was that he was, unfortunately, right.

"What happened between us was a by-product of grief, that's all."

He said nothing. Clara's nerves began to fray under his steady gaze. She was no good at this. She had no experience in it. It sounded as if *she* was giving *him* the brush-off, which was ridiculous, wasn't it?

"I didn't ask you out here so we could replay our mistakes," he said softly. "Though for my part, I don't have any regrets. I hope you don't either, Clara. I never wanted to hurt you, or take advantage of you in any way."

"You didn't," she whispered. If anything she felt as

though she'd taken advantage of him. "You were a gentleman from the first, Ty."

"I didn't know how to act around you. I knew what you'd been through and I never knew if I should touch you or turn away, talk about it or ignore it. I just knew things were better when you were around. You made me understand a lot of things, and because of it I was able to make amends with my dad. So thank you, Clara." He reached out and pulled her hand out of her pocket, folding it within his, warm even through his glove and her mitten. "I hope your new life is everything you wanted. I am so glad that you're reconnecting with your family because I know how important that is. And I hope you'll look back on your time at Diamondback as something good and positive and not colored by the last week."

A stinging began behind her nose. This really was goodbye, then. She hated that a part of her heart had wanted him to say something more sentimental. Hated knowing that she might have reconsidered leaving if he'd admitted he'd fallen in love with her the way she'd fallen for him. But he didn't. Because he'd been honest, right? Ty didn't fall in love. He'd told her that at the very beginning.

"Of course I will," she answered, unable to stop the quiver in her voice.

"I'm so happy for you. It's a whole new start, and you'll have your family back. But I'll miss you, Clara. I wanted you to know that before you went. I'll miss you."

She clenched her teeth together, trying to hold her emotions in, but they got the better of her. Her lower lip began to wobble as she looked up...and he took off his hat.

His eyes. Oh, his eyes were dark and tortured and she thought for a minute that he might reach out and pull her close and tell her it was all a mistake. But he didn't. Instead he held out his hand, offering it to her to shake. She stared at it, not wanting to take it. It seemed less than it should be between them somehow. And to not take it would leave such a bitter taste for both of them. She couldn't let things end that way. Not after all he'd given to her. All the things she couldn't say. He'd given her back her confidence, he'd taken away her fear with his gentleness. He'd taught her to laugh again and made her feel as though she had something unique to offer the world. He'd done all of that simply by being Ty.

So she held out her hand, put it in his and felt her insides tremble.

"Good luck with Diamondback, Ty. You and Sam are going to do great things, I just know it."

Her gaze landed on his lips. She'd done so well by coming out with a platonic wish for the future. But then she'd looked at his lips, and then back to his eyes, and everything they'd been holding back seemed to sizzle between them again.

He squeezed her fingers almost painfully. "And good luck to you, Clara, and your shiny new life. If anyone deserves it, you do."

One of them had to let go. One of them had to make the first move and slide their fingers out of the clasp. And yet it went on, and on, hovering on the brink of becoming more, holding back.

Finally Ty pulled his hand from hers and put his hat on his head. The lump in her throat got bigger as silently he tipped a finger to the brim and then reached for the door handle of the truck.

Then he paused, left the truck door open, came back and pressed a kiss to her cheek. His lips were warm and soft, and she desperately wanted to pull him to her and just tell him how she felt and ask if she could stay.

It was only the crushing realization that her feelings

wouldn't be returned that held her back from confessing it all. And if she did, she'd know that once more she wouldn't be making the smart decision for her life but the one based on her feelings for a man who didn't feel the same way about her.

"Goodbye, Clara," he murmured, and she closed her eyes, imprinting the feel of his lips, the warmth of his breath, the masculine scent of him on her brain one last time.

"'Bye, Tyson."

He hopped into the cab of the truck and started the engine as she stepped back onto the shoulder of the road, out of the way.

Then he was gone in a cloud of exhaust. And she was left standing there, on the brink of a whole new shiny life that suddenly didn't feel quite as shiny as it ought.

CHAPTER TEN

A WARM CHINOOK had come over the Rockies, pushing through Alberta into Saskatchewan and providing an uncharacteristic springlike feeling to the air considering it was only February.

Clara parked the car in the garage and shut off the key, resting her head on the steering wheel for a moment. She was so tired lately, and getting up in the night to pee wasn't helping her much either. She often got back in bed and couldn't nod off again as she kept thinking about Ty, and Diamondback, and the consequences she hadn't seen coming from their night together.

She was going to have to tell him. Soon. This was not something she could keep a secret. Ty deserved to know he was going to be a father. She'd only held off this long because she'd wanted to be sure.

She'd wanted to get through the first trimester safely before sharing the news. And she'd wanted to give herself a little time to think—to sort out her feelings and make some sort of plan. There was no question about going through with the pregnancy. She'd already been given one second chance in her life and she wasn't about to squander another. But that in itself created so many questions that the more she tried to sort things out, the more confused she became.

The door connecting the garage to the house opened. "Clara, you coming in?"

She looked up at her mother, holding the door open. Wendy's face was creased with concern. Clara hadn't been able to keep the pregnancy secret for long once morning sickness kicked in, and the whole story had come tumbling out. She'd forgotten how wonderful it was to be held in her mother's arms and told it would all be okay. But she also knew that her mother worried about her plenty. She dropped the keys into her purse and slung it over her shoulder as she opened the car door. "Sorry."

"Dinner's almost ready. Beef stew and spinach salad."

Clara's stomach growled at the good news. "Lots of iron. Maybe that's what I've been craving lately."

Wendy Ferguson shrugged. "Gotta keep you and that little one fed." She smiled. "Oh, and that friend of yours called. Angela? She asked if you'd call her back at her house. I told her I'd pass on the message."

Clara's appetite took a nose dive. What did Angela want? For the first month they'd kept in touch briefly. Part of that was Angela keeping tabs on people who had gone through her program. But now it was different. Clara didn't like keeping secrets, and talking to Angela did nothing more than remind her of Diamondback and Cadence Creek and how much she missed them all.

"I'll call her later. Thanks for making dinner again."

"Your turn's coming. I'm back to work on Monday."

They'd been doing a fair job of splitting the housekeeping duties, with whoever was home taking over cooking meals and throwing in a load of laundry when time allowed. For Clara, it was more like having a roommate than living at home with a parent, and for that she was glad. Reconnecting with her mother had helped fill a space that had been empty for a long time. She'd been welcomed back with open arms and a few tears. She'd even spoken to her brother on the phone, all the way from where he was living in Australia. Bit by bit she was getting back the pieces of her life that had been scattered.

All except one. Her feelings for Ty hadn't dimmed in the least. How were they ever going to manage to parent this child with everything so complicated?

Once dinner was over she grabbed the phone and went to her room to talk to Angela in private. Perhaps it was nothing, just a follow-up from the Butterfly Foundation as usual. Angela answered on the first ring and Clara laughed. "Were you sitting on the phone?"

"Just about," Angela said. "It's good to hear your voice, Clara."

"You, too," she answered, and it really was. Angela had been more than her social worker. They'd been friends. She'd been Angela's bridesmaid, after all, and along with Ty and Molly she missed Angela, too. Looking back, Clara supposed it was odd that she'd never confided to Angela that she'd developed feelings for Ty. But then it had been pretty obvious, hadn't it? And while no one had breathed a word about seeing her car in the drive the morning after the funeral, Clara knew it was foolish to think no one had noticed.

"I'm calling with a specific invitation," Angela chirped. "Molly's birthday. It's coming up a week from Monday, but we're having a party on Saturday night to celebrate. Just a few close friends for dinner at the new house. Tell me you have the weekend off."

She did, so there was that excuse out the window. She hesitated, searching for an excuse not to go. "It's an awfully long drive, Ang, and it's still winter."

"Well, we can't control that. If it's storming, you won't come of course. But otherwise you will, right?"

She needed to see Ty, but this was not how she wanted to do it. She wanted it to be on her own time, in her own way, when she was ready and with a clear plan. "I don't know…"

"Come on, you can stay here. We finally have a real spare room and you can be our first guest. Or you can stay at the ranch. Though Ty's there…"

"What's that supposed to mean?" She asked the question before she could stop herself.

"Just that, well, things seemed kind of tense between you before you left. Did you argue or something?"

Tense didn't begin to cover it. Clara had fallen in love with a man who didn't love her back.

"There was a lot going on, that's all." She tried to pass it off as nothing. "There are no hard feelings or anything."

"Then you'll come?"

Clara thought for a moment. What better excuse would she have for driving all the way to Cadence Creek? And she did have to tell Ty about the baby. Soon. It wouldn't do to show up at his door in maternity clothes or carrying a car seat with a bundle of joy. They should talk now so they had lots of time to make calm, rational decisions.

"Would it be okay if I came on Friday?" That way she could talk to Ty privately, beforehand.

"I'd love that! Let's pray for good weather and I'll see you then."

"See you," Clara echoed, as they finished the conversation and hung up.

A week. She had barely a week to come up with a plan that would allow her to raise her baby, allow Ty to be a father, and keep her heart intact.

Easy peasy, she thought skeptically, sinking back onto

the pillows of her bed and wondering why the nausea, which had been so much better this week, was suddenly back.

The Chinook of the previous week had missed Cadence Creek, and the fields were still blanketed with white as Clara drove past the main house and headed to Sam and Angela's. The two-story Cape Cod was welcoming, with lights glowing through the windows as afternoon waned. It had taken Clara most of the day to get here, and she was looking forward to stretching her legs in a big way.

And she had to find a way to talk to Ty. Maybe in the morning, when they were both fresh and she'd had a chance to sleep on the words she was preparing to say. She'd decided she wanted to stay close to Moose Jaw, with her mother, at least for the time being. She'd have wonderful support and flexible hours working at the local hospital. She hoped Ty would support her in her decision, especially when she told him that she wanted him to be involved as much as possible. It wouldn't always be easy, but surely they could work out visitation. They were adults, after all.

She knocked on the door, carrying her overnight bag on her shoulder. First she needed to pee—pregnancy bladder was killer—and freshen up her makeup. She wanted to be completely prepared and collected when she saw him again.

She was firmly in control when the door opened. And that control went sideways when Ty stood in the breach.

"You!" she said, and her bag slipped off her shoulder and hit the step with a thump.

"Hi to you, too," he said. Oh, how she'd missed that voice. A little soft, a little smooth, completely masculine.

Her mouth opened and closed a few times, and all her

practiced words flew out of her head. He was here. Right now. Looking the way he always did—careless, casual and gorgeous.

And his baby was inside her.

She reached down and picked up her bag, willing her hands not to tremble and taking calming breaths. When she straightened her head got a little fuzzy, as it often did when she made quick changes in position these days. She forced a smile. "May I come in, then? It's cold out here."

He stood aside and opened the door so she could enter the foyer.

The house was new and quite grand by Clara's standards, all wide, white woodwork and polished hardwood and gleaming light fixtures. "I thought Angela would be here," she said, hearing her voice echo in the vaulted hallway.

"She's just popped up out to the diner for pie for dessert."

The diner. Clara felt a familiar twist in her stomach thinking of that night and how Ty had smiled at her and talked about Virgil. She remembered too how she'd put her fingers on his when he'd explained how he came to be at Diamondback as a baby. Their closeness had really begun that night, hadn't it?

"So you're staying for dinner?" She chanced a look up at him.

He nodded. "I was invited. But if it makes you too uncomfortable…"

The front door opened and Angela stepped through, her cheeks rosy and a paper sack balanced in her hands. "You're here! Yay! Let me put this in the kitchen and come back and hug you properly!"

She hurried through to the kitchen and Clara raised an eyebrow. "She's so, wow. Excited? Bubbly." It was more than that. Angela was so open with her affection now. Angela had fought her own demons and won, but she'd still had a bit of reserve that kept her at arm's length some of the time. That seemed to be completely gone. "I've never seen her like this."

"I think it's called happiness," Ty remarked dryly.

"Do you suppose it's catching?"

"I guess we can hope, right? It looks good on her."

She smiled, a genuine smile this time rather than strained politeness. This was the Ty she'd liked from the start. Easygoing, charming, with a ready smile.

Angela bustled back and enveloped Clara in a welcoming hug. "You look great," she said. "Doesn't she look great, Ty?"

Angela was fishing now and Clara felt heat rise in her cheeks. "Great," Ty said quietly, and her eyes found his immediately. The warm brown depths held a gleam of approval that sent her heart thumping in an all-too-familiar way. This was what was going to make it difficult, wasn't it? Her feelings hadn't changed. And it was going to be hell trying to keep them out of the way.

"Come on in the kitchen and tell me what you've really been up to," Angela suggested, taking Clara by the hand. "Ty, why don't you find out what's keeping Sam? Dinner's in half an hour."

"If that's your not-so-subtle invitation to get out of the way so you can have some girl-talk, I accept," Ty replied, flashing a grin. "And I'll make sure Sam's here on time."

Clara was tugged away towards the kitchen and as they entered the large room, she slipped her hand out of Angela's. "Can you point me in the direction of the bathroom? It was a long drive."

"Oh, look at me! Of course. And let me show you to

your room instead. You can freshen up or whatever until dinner. I'm sorry, I'm just so happy to see you again."

"I'm happy to see you, too," Clara admitted. Being here felt like coming home—was it possible for someone to have two homes?

Angela changed direction, taking Clara upstairs instead as she kept chattering. "We'll have plenty of time to catch up later." She stopped in front of a white door. "We can curl up on the sofa with hot cocoa tonight and whisper to our heart's content."

She opened the door. The room was beautiful. Clara stepped inside, putting her bag on the floor at the foot of the bed before spinning around. "Oh, Angela. You must love your house."

"I do. It's exactly what I always dreamed of, even as a kid. I'm so lucky. So happy." She leaned against the door and smiled wistfully. "And you. You're back home with your mom. It's good, right?"

"It's been wonderful. All the things I remembered, though the house is different now because she moved into a townhouse, and some of those good things are just memories. But she kept a lot of the things I remember and she hasn't changed a bit. I feel like I got myself back, Ang, and that's all thanks to you."

"Nonsense. But I'm so happy for you. I won't lie—we miss you around here. Anyway, there's an ensuite through that door that's yours. Take your time."

When she was gone, Clara explored the ensuite and freshened up, then perched on the window seat for a few moments, staring out the window. It overlooked the gate and driveway and she saw Sam and Ty drive in, and Ty's long legs as he hopped out of the truck. She wondered what he would say when she told him. He didn't want kids of his own, did he? He'd said that he'd never want to be in the position his birth parents had found themselves. That he'd always been careful.

But they hadn't been careful, had they? They'd been reckless and emotional. Fine beginning for a child. Her head began to ache and she knew she had to find a way to speak to Ty soon. Dragging it out wasn't going to help at all. Once dinner was over and the dishes tucked away into the dishwasher, Clara touched Angela's arm. "I need a favor."

"Of course. Name it."

Clara met Angela's gaze. "I'll explain later, I promise, okay? Is there a place where I can speak to Ty? Alone?"

"You can use my office. Are you okay?"

Clara lifted her shoulders and dropped them again. "To be honest? I don't know. But I have a feeling I'll need that cocoa later, okay?"

"You got it." Angela squeezed her shoulder. "He's a good man, Clara. And I think he's been a bit lost since you left."

Oh, that was not what she wanted to hear! She swallowed against the unease building in her throat. "Thanks, Ang." She went to the door of the living room and cleared her throat. "Ty?" she asked. "Could I have a word?"

"Sure," he replied, surprise blanking his face but he rose instantly.

"Angela said we could use her office."

There was a hint of alarm flattening his features now and his eyes, usually twinkling with mischief, darkened with concern. "Lead the way," he said, standing beside her shoulder.

She shut the door behind them and closed her eyes, taking a restorative breath.

"What's wrong?" He was in front of her in an instant. "You're pale, and you've had this funny look since you arrived. Are you sick? Is everything okay in Moose Jaw? Are you in trouble?"

Oh, Lord, his genuine concern was almost too much to bear. Then he put his hands on her upper arms, rubbing his thumbs along the surface of her shirt and creating a lovely warm friction beneath his touch. She blinked a few times—she was determined to get through this conversation without turning into a waterworks. "I'm not in trouble. Not the way you're thinking, anyway." She tried to smile but it felt crooked and odd. "I've got a good job, and sharing a condo with my mom has been wonderful. Truly."

"Then what is it?" He squatted down a bit and looked her dead in the eye. "Why do you need to talk to me alone?"

His cheeks turned slightly ruddy. My goodness, was Ty Diamond blushing?

"If it's about the last night you were here…what I said… is it…" He cleared his throat roughly. "Do you still have feelings for me? I swear I didn't mean to hurt you, Clara, I…"

She slid out of his grasp and took a few stumbling steps. "No! I mean, that's not why I wanted to talk to you," she amended, feeling the conversation already getting off track. She faced him and lifted her chin as much as she dared, gathering all her strength and composure. "Ty, about the night we spent together…"

He stilled.

She locked her gaze with his. "We didn't use any protection, Ty," she said gently. "And I'm pregnant."

For the space of a second his eyes widened and his lips dropped open. Then he put a hand over his mouth and scraped it along his chin as he absorbed the hit.

"Pregnant."

"I was as surprised as you are."

"When did you… How long have you known?"

"Since before Christmas."

His gaze narrowed. "And you waited until now, why?"

This was the hard part, wasn't it? The real reason she had kept the news to herself. It wasn't just about her feelings for Ty, but her own insecurity and guilt and the resulting fear. It was finding out the news and feeling happy and terrified and confused and wanting to cherish the knowledge and keep it to herself in case something went horribly wrong.

The last time she'd thought being pregnant would fix things, but she'd been younger and her thinking had been skewed and she'd been so utterly wrong. She was older now. She knew better. And so she'd held the secret inside until her conscience told her she couldn't anymore.

"I…I…" She hated that she sounded so weak. "I didn't know how, Ty. It was such a shock at first. And you'd just lost your father. The last thing you needed was more upheaval. But you deserve to know. Angela's invitation came and I knew I couldn't keep you in the dark any longer."

"Oh, man," he breathed, sinking down on the futon next to the wall. "I'm going to be a father."

"I know it's a shock."

"You've got that right."

She wanted to go sit beside him but didn't. She needed the distance to keep her perspective. To stay strong. That wouldn't happen if she sat beside him. He'd be too close. She was already far too aware of everything about him.

"I've thought about it, Ty, and I definitely want you to be part of this baby's life." She tried to smile. "I've got things pretty good now—my mom's been wonderful and I have a great new job. I won't be without any support this…" She broke off the sentence, a tiny pain clutching at her heart. "Anyway, I'm ready to raise him. Or her. And

I know we can work it out so you can see him—or her—
whenever you want. We're grown-ups. We can…"

"Like hell," he interrupted, standing. "I can see the baby
whenever I want?" His lip curled. "How long did you re-
hearse, Clara? Did you really think you could sell me on
this farce of a parenting proposal?"

Hope plummeted. "But you don't even want to be a
parent!"

"What I wanted and what's to be are two very different things. You know that." He went to her and gripped
her wrist. "How could you ever think that I'd let my own
child be raised miles away, to see them what, a few times
a year? A week in the summer and every other Christmas?" His eyes blazed at her now, sparking with indigna-
tion. "No child of mine will ever feel unwanted or pushed
aside! After all you know about me. After all I told you.
I'd never told anyone before, did you know that?" He let
go of her wrist, pushing it aside as if it were distasteful.
"I thought you knew me better than that. I thought I knew
you better than that."

The insult hit its mark and she inhaled sharply. "That's
not fair. Neither of us planned this! What am I supposed
to do, Ty? I just found my family again. I just started over
with a job and a whole new life!"

"So you don't want it?"

Hurt seemed to seep through her, right through her
very bones. She went to a meeting chair and perched on
the edge, trying to catch her breath. "I want it so much I
can hardly stand it," she whispered. She hated that he was
angry. Hated that this was the situation her baby would
grow up in. There should be harmony, not conflict. Working together, not against each other. "Oh, Ty," she breathed.
"I have had so many second chances. I'm so afraid of
blowing this one. I always thought I'd be too afraid to be

pregnant again, but now I am and it's the most terrifying, humbling, wonderful thing. I know we can find a way to work this out. We have to, don't you see?"

Ty had grown dangerously quiet. "Again?" he asked softly.

Panic blossomed. She'd said that, hadn't she? She'd said the word *again* when Ty didn't know about before. How could he? It was *her* deep, dark secret.

And finally the strain was too much to bear. She put her face in her hands and began to cry.

Ty hadn't expected tears. He hadn't expected any of this. When she'd called him in here tonight, he'd seriously thought she'd found herself in trouble again and needed his help. That perhaps she hadn't quite been ready to go it alone as she thought.

But a baby? His baby. As he'd stared at her, he'd flashed back to that night in the barn when it had been conceived. There had been grief, but there'd been more than that, too. It had been beautiful, and right, and for the first time ever, Ty had let himself give up emotional control when with a woman. He'd bared himself to her in a way he'd never done before. He doubted she knew that.

There'd been no one since either.

He knelt beside her and touched her hair. "Tell me what you mean by 'again,'" he said quietly. There were layers to Clara he still hadn't unwrapped. Things he figured he should know before this went any further.

She didn't answer, and he saw a tear sneak below her palms, dropping off her chin to the rug below her chair. It damn near ripped him apart to see her cry. Clara, the cheerful one. Clara, the woman who looked after everyone else. She was weeping quietly as if her heart would break, and even though the whole thing was a damned mess, he gathered her in his arms and let her cry it out.

"Clara," he finally nudged gently. "You're killing my legs here. Let's sit on the futon."

She nodded against his shirt and stood, shaky at first, as he pushed up out of the crouch and led her to the futon. She sat, avoiding his gaze. Her face was red and puffy from crying and her hair was a tangle around her cheeks, the odd strand stuck to the skin with tears. She was still the most beautiful woman he knew. More beautiful now that she was carrying his child. But she wanted to raise it a province away without him. He couldn't let that happen. What was she afraid of? He was sure that was the key to everything.

"Can you tell me now?" he asked, rubbing her hand between his. "What did you mean by again? Do you have another child, Clara?"

"Do you see another?" She wrinkled her brow. "That question doesn't make sense."

"Sure it does. You might have given one up for adoption. Is that what you meant by a second chance?"

She shook her head. "No. The decision was taken out of my hands." Again she paused. And sighed. "I've never told anyone this. Not even Angela. Oh, Tyson, it's so hard."

"Just say it," he said. "I need to know, Clara."

"Yes, you do." She sounded resigned as she leaned back against the cushion of the futon. "It was when I was with Jackson, you see. I found out I was pregnant. I thought if he knew that maybe he'd let up, you know? He'd been so good to me at first. I thought maybe it could be that way again." She met Ty's gaze with sad eyes. "I know now how stupid that sounds."

"Not stupid," Ty murmured. "Desperate."

"Well, regardless, I was wrong. He flew into a rage.

Said it wasn't his, and accused me of sleeping around."
Bitterness crept into her voice. "When would I have time
to do that? When I wasn't at work, he practically kept me
under lock and key."

"He beat you when you were pregnant?"

"Three fractured ribs and a broken nose and a lot of
bruises. And a miscarriage."

Ty felt as if someone had punched him in the gut. Even
suspecting what was coming, he couldn't comprehend a
man who could do that to a woman. Not when she was
carrying a precious baby inside her. All the air came out
of his lungs and he gripped her fingers tighter.

"So now you understand," she whispered, "why I want
it so much. Why I want to do it right this time. I couldn't
tell you before because I wanted to get past the first trimester and be sure things were okay. I needed to wrap
my head around the idea of being a mom and being me."

Nothing about sorting out her feelings for him, then.
He knew he shouldn't be hurt by that. They'd had a one-
night thing during an emotional storm. They'd cared for
each other but neither of them had used the word *love,*
had they? Clara had always made it clear that she wanted
her own life and her independence, and it appeared she
was still determined to have it. If he admitted he loved
her now, wouldn't she think he was trying to manipulate
her to get his way?

Would he be? His head was spinning so much right
now that he couldn't even be sure. All he knew was that
no child of his would be raised without him there every
step of the way.

There could be no solution tonight. Clara looked exhausted and he wasn't sure where to go next. He looked
at where her shirt lay over the zipper of her jeans and his
heart gave a little kick. His baby was in there. The one

they'd created together. And that baby deserved better than this.

"May I?" He held out his hand, letting it hover over her tummy. He wished he didn't have to ask. Wished that things were different, that they'd gotten the news together, that they'd shared in it and worried about it as one. But they hadn't, because none of this had been supposed to happen. Now they just had to roll with it, right?

She nodded. "Yes, of course."

He put his hand on her still-flat belly. "There's no bump there yet," he murmured, the warmth from her body seeping into his palm.

"Soon," she replied. "My waistbands are already getting a little tight. Thank God scrubs have drawstrings."

He should remove his hand but it felt too good. Instead he looked into her face. It hit him then, with the force of a brick upside the head. He *did* love her. Not just love... He was *in* love with her. All the way, headfirst without a safety net, in love with her. With her sweetness, with her tender heart, with the life she carried inside her. Nothing in his life—not even the first moment when she'd said the words *I'm pregnant*—had frightened and exhilarated him this way. How could a man feel as though he could take on the world and be so terrified of failure at the same time?

"Nothing needs to be decided tonight," he said, finally sliding his hand off her tummy. "We both need time to think. I know we can work this out, Clara. We both want to do what's right, and that means we will. Somehow."

"I wish I had your confidence. Some people might find it cocky, but I admire that."

"We'll make a good team," he replied, the beginnings of something flickering inside, expanding into a glow of certainty. "You care about people, Clara. You always have, even when you were hurt and distrustful. You'll make a wonderful mother."

"I appreciate that more than you know."

"It'll be okay," he said, stronger. "I have a lot to think about, and you need some rest, right? I'll see you tomorrow for the party?"

"Of course."

"And you'll be okay now?"

"Ty." She smiled. It was good to see her smile without the strain that had been around her eyes since…well, since the night they'd spent together, if he were being truthful. "I've had longer to get used to the idea. It's okay to freak a little."

He leaned down and kissed her forehead, wondering what she'd say if she really knew what he was thinking. "I'll see you tomorrow, then."

He left the office and headed straight to the foyer. His head was swimming with so many things right now—pregnancy and fatherhood and being in love and how to make it all come together in the right way without sending Clara running in a panic. He wished his father was there to talk to. Virgil would have known what to do. He wouldn't have minced words either. Ty had hated that bluntness for years, and had hated that Virgil always seemed to be right as well.

But right now he missed what he realized had been guidance and love all along.

"Ty? Is everything okay?"

Angela stopped at the end of the hall and folded her arms, a look of concern wrinkling her features.

"It will be," he answered. He nodded towards the office. "Clara could use a friend, though."

Angela came forward. "I knew something was wrong. She was far too quiet at dinner. Is she okay?"

"Don't worry," Ty said, wishing he felt more of the confidence Clara seemed so sure he possessed. "I'm going to make everything right."

As he stepped out into the frigid air, he turned up his collar. He would come up with the solution. And he'd do it before Clara left on Sunday.

CHAPTER ELEVEN

CLARA SIGHED WITH frustration as she tried to button the trousers she'd brought for the party. Things were starting to not fit. The faint bubble of her belly wasn't really visible, but it would be soon. Especially if she were popping buttons and zippers all over the place.

The button finally went through the hole and she frowned, looking at the reflection in the mirror. Thank goodness she'd brought a flowing kind of blouse to wear over top. It would cover the ill-fitting waistband. She put her hands over her tummy, and the frown slid from her face. Things were so very complicated but she couldn't find it within herself to be sorry. She was going to be a mother. And she was going to do everything possible to be a good one. She'd make the right decisions this time.

Except there was the small matter of Ty to consider. She got the feeling he'd have ideas of his own. And she also got the feeling that he might not go along with her plans as easily as she hoped.

Angela knocked on the door and stuck her head inside. "You ready to go?"

Clara nodded. "As ready as I'm going to be." She picked up her purse and followed Angela down the stairs. "You're not going to say anything to Molly, right?" Angela had been so concerned last night that Clara had confessed about the pregnancy. Angela had been shocked but not totally surprised that something had happened between Clara and Ty. "Ty and I need to talk before anyone else is brought into it. You understand."

"Of course I do. I won't breathe a word."

The drive to the main house was short and Clara swallowed thickly as they approached the house. She'd done a lot of growing here. She'd found her heart again at Diamondback. Moving back to Moose Jaw had been the right decision, and it had given her something back that had been missing.

But Diamondback...it felt like home.

Molly met them at the door, and before Clara could catch a breath, she found herself enveloped in a tight hug. "My goodness, girl," Molly said, stepping back and grinning from ear to ear. "It's good to see you. You look wonderful. Just glowing."

Buster bounced around, barking and offering his own doggy greeting with wags of his tail. Clara nearly swallowed her tongue but recovered quickly. "It's the winter air putting roses in my cheeks. How are you, Molly?"

"I'm doing okay. House seems awful big these days. But Ty's here. I can't be lonely when I have family all around, can I?" She looked at Angela and raised an eyebrow. "Now all I need are a few grandbabies to cuddle."

Clara scurried aside, hiding her face as she unbuttoned her coat and hung it on her customary peg behind the door. Molly couldn't possibly have said anything that would make her more uncomfortable. Even Angela had an odd, tight look on her face, but at least that could be explained away by being put on the spot.

"What's the rush?" Sam interjected smoothly, giving his mother a kiss on the cheek. He winked at Clara. "Where's Ty? I figured he'd be where the cake is."

The timing of the question was perfect as Ty stomped in, clearing the light snow from his boots. "Someone ask for me?" he grinned. "I was on food duty, remember?" He held up a gigantic paper bag. "Mom requested Chinese. The birthday girl gets her wish."

Molly took the bag from him and put it on the butcher block. "We'll have to heat this up a bit, but it won't take long."

Angela and Sam went to help, and Ty turned his attention towards Clara. His gaze was warm and soft as he looked at her, and she felt herself turning to jelly. He'd always been able to do that, right from the first. And now there was something more in that light of approval in his eyes. There was the knowing. Knowing each other intimately. Knowing they'd created another human being. It was a powerful force.

"Clara," he said simply, and her heart turned over.

"Hi," she replied softly, watching as he took off his jacket, hanging it beside hers. He looked so good, maybe even better than she remembered. The tan brushed-cotton of his shirt brought out the glints of gold in his eyes, and it fit across the breadth of his shoulders as if it had been tailored for him. With a stutter of her heart she realized that she hoped she had a boy just like him—big brown eyes and a lightning grin and a mop of stubborn dark hair.

"How'd you sleep last night?" He stepped closer and kept his voice low, letting the chatter behind him provide a little bit of cover.

But now he was very near and her pulse started leaping around. Why couldn't she keep her reactions to him under control? Co-parenting was going to be hellish if this kept getting in the way. Maybe it would get better in time. It had to, right?

"Okay." She tried a smile. "To be honest, I've been worrying so much about telling you that I think I slept better because it was such a relief to have it over with."

She looked over his shoulder; Sam and Molly and Angela were still putting food in dishes and there was a steady hum as Angela started the microwave.

"How about you?" she asked.

"Not so good. I did a lot of thinking."

"I'm sorry."

"Don't be." He frowned, then pinned her with a direct gaze. "Things won't be ready for a while. Can we talk? Somewhere more private than the living room?"

"Sure," she answered. Not that she was in any hurry to be alone with Ty, but she sure as heck didn't want them to be overheard either.

He led her through the living room and up the stairs. "I hope this isn't awkward," he said. "My room is probably the best place to avoid being interrupted."

His room? Clara paused, but what else could she do? He was right. Anywhere downstairs they'd risk being interrupted or overheard. She stepped inside when he opened the door and took a fortifying breath.

The door shut with a quiet click and Clara immediately felt the intimacy of being closed away in his personal space. The bed was made of sturdy pine and covered with one of Molly's handmade quilts in cozy shades of tan and chocolate and cream. A sturdy shelf covered one wall and was full of huge trophies and accolades. Goodness, he had been successful, hadn't he? It seemed a little bit glamorous to Clara and there was a sense of awe in knowing this was the sort of man who'd fathered her child.

His window overlooked the north pasture and the view extended for miles, the odd house and barn of neighboring ranches dotting the rolling landscape here and there. From this view Clara truly began to realize how big Diamondback was. What a responsibility it was for Sam and Ty, and her respect for them both—and for Virgil—grew.

She turned away from the window and faced him. The bed was behind her and she had the persistent thought that it was quite inappropriate, under the circumstances, to be so very aware of it. To be aware of him. She wanted to be in his arms. To feel his lips on hers once more. Oh, how she'd missed that. But it went against everything she wanted to accomplish, so she clasped her hands together, bit down on her lip and waited. Last night she'd said her piece. Clearly Ty wanted to say his.

"You're nervous," he said gently, standing just in front of the door. Not moving any closer, but not getting any farther away either.

"I'm fine," she contradicted, but he shook his head.

"You always bite down on your lip when you're uncomfortable, did you know that? It's quite attractive, actually."

"Ty…"

This time he took a step forward. "I thought about it all night, Clara. Thought about you and the baby and Diamondback, and I know what we have to do."

She wasn't sure she liked the sound of this. He seemed very sure of himself, and considering she'd already explained her proposal this meant he wasn't likely to go along with it. She tangled her fingers tighter together and replied as evenly as she could, "I already told you what I'd like to do. This doesn't have to change anything, not really. I can keep my life and you can keep yours, and we can work it out so that our baby has both a mother and a father. Right?"

Somehow in the twisting of her fingers, she managed to cross hers, hoping he would see reason.

Another step closer, and this time he was shaking his head. "That doesn't work for me, Clara. I can't be a father from hundreds of kilometers away." He reached out and pried one of her hands loose, clasping it in his strong, warm fingers. "What makes the most sense is…"

He paused, then got down on one knee while her mouth fell open. No, no, no! This couldn't be happening. He couldn't possibly be proposing. It would ruin everything! She didn't want to get married. Didn't want to lose herself in another relationship where she wasn't loved in return. Why couldn't he just be reasonable?

She tried to slide her fingers out of his but his grip was too firm. Oh, God, he was looking up at her with those heart-on-his-sleeve eyes and she couldn't look away.

"I want you to marry me," he said softly. "Come home to Diamondback, and we can raise our child together."

Panic threaded its way through her body. "We don't have to get married to be parents," she answered, adding a nervous laugh to the end that fell completely flat. Ty's brow furrowed and a wrinkle appeared just above his nose.

He got to his feet and Clara realized once more how very tall he was. Ty had such presence that he tended to fill a room with it without even trying. It was hard to go toe-to-toe with that. But the truth was Ty had mentioned absolutely nothing about love. He had asked her, but for all the wrong reasons. And it would be a disaster to marry without it. They would end up resenting each other and then what sort of parents would they be?

She had to make him understand that somehow. "Ty," she tried, praying for calm, "getting married would be a mistake. We'd end up regretting it, I'm sure of it. And then there'd be a child stuck in the middle. If we're calm and practical now, it'll be so much better, can't you see? We'll make rational decisions rather than running on emotion."

"Of course there are emotions involved. We're not talk-

ing about buying a car or taking a job. We're talking about
a baby here. My baby."

"And mine," she reminded him.

A muscle in his jaw ticked. This wasn't going the way
she wanted at all! It had never crossed her mind that he'd
propose. He didn't love her. She wasn't a naive little girl,
after all. She knew that one night of passion and grief did
not a love affair make.

"You're asking me to make an impossible choice, do
you realize that?" He ran his hand through his hair. "I
either have to try to be a father on special occasions and
holidays, or…"

He dropped his hand. "Damn," he muttered.

"Or what?" she asked, wondering what choice she'd
possibly forced.

"Or leave Diamondback."

Her lips dropped open. "You'd do that?"

The chocolaty eyes she'd drowned in earlier now hard-
ened. "What choice would I have? You should know me
better, especially after everything I told you." His voice
turned accusing. "You know my history. You know how
I feel about what my parents did. Thank God Virgil and
Molly were there, but what if they hadn't been? Don't you
think I know how it might have ended up for me? Maybe
this was unplanned, but I could never turn my back on my
own child. I could never put them second in my life and I
thought you understood that."

And now she saw his eyes glisten with the barest sheen
of moisture before he blinked and turned away from her.

"But you love Diamondback," she said weakly.

"Yes, I do." His voice was hoarse with emotion. And he
didn't need to say anything more. If she insisted on staying in Saskatchewan, he would leave the ranch behind.
His birthright. His family.

"All last night I asked myself what my dad would do in my place," he said. He faced her once more, the harsh anger gone from his features but replaced by naked anguish. "I wished I had him to talk to. But in the end I knew what he'd do. Because he'd already done it—with me. He put me first. He'd done what was best and that was give me a family and security and love. Our baby deserves at least that much. I blew my chance with my father too many times to count. You're not the only one with a second chance, Clara. I wasn't the best son, but I can damn well be a good father. I know in my heart the best way to do that is for us to make a home here, at Diamondback. To be a real family."

Clara's resolve was weakening and she knew she had to say the word they were both so assiduously avoiding. "How can you be a real family without love?" she asked.

A shadow passed over his face. "We'll have love for our child," he replied. "And maybe for us, too, in time." He offered a weak smile. "Haven't we always gotten along? I mean, we wouldn't be here if we didn't. Maybe we just need to give it time."

Her heart wept a little. This was not the way marriage was supposed to start out.

Was it enough? She knew it wasn't. And yet how could she ask him to give up Diamondback without at least compromising? She knew they weren't idle words on Ty's part. He was determined and stubborn and he'd do it. He'd leave Diamondback and he'd be a good father but miserable.

And there was the niggling reminder that she loved it here. She was happy she had her family back in her life and she liked her job, but this felt like home. She'd be stupid to deny it.

"I don't know, Ty."

He sensed her weakening and hit her with one more

emotional shot: "It would kill Mom to have you both so far away. She's already started bugging Sam and Angela about babies. She's wanted grandchildren for years. With Dad gone now this would be so good for her, Clara."

"What if it doesn't work out? What if…"

Ty stepped forward and cupped her face in his hands. "It will. I promise. It's too important not to."

He touched his lips to hers, a faint whisper of contact but it rocketed through Clara like a lightning bolt.

"Marry me," he murmured against her lips.

She nodded. How could she resist when deep down Ty was what she really wanted? How could she say no when her only reasoning was to prove a point? How could she ask him to give everything up so she could be selfish and have her own way?

And perhaps she'd learn how to swallow her fear and believe that one day he might come to love her, too.

When they entered the kitchen again, three pairs of eyes watched them curiously. Clara felt her cheeks heat as she realized they'd been gone several minutes and that they'd kept the meal waiting. Angela sent Clara a sympathetic look and Sam was grinning at Ty like an idiot. Molly's face, however, had fallen into wrinkles of concern. "Is everything all right?" she asked.

"Fine," Clara answered before Ty could get a chance. "Sorry we held you up. Everything smells delicious." Truthfully she didn't care a bit about eating but she'd put on a good show. Anything to put things back to normal.

Angela gave Molly a plate and everyone dished up the food buffet-style, but even though snatches of conversation picked up, the atmosphere remained strained. They sat at the table and Clara saw Angela give Sam a kick. He winced and then picked up his water glass. "Well, I sup-

pose we should kick off the festivities. How about a toast?"
He beamed at the table in general. "To Mom, on her birthday." Everyone clinked glasses and drank, but Sam wasn't
done yet. "And to family. All of us being together."

Ty grinned at his brother, and Angela aimed a per-
turbed look at him; poor Molly only looked confused.
"All right," she said, putting down her glass. "Would one
of you care to tell me what's going on here? The atmosphere's so thick you could cut it with a knife and I know
I'm completely in the dark."

Clara froze. Ty reached over and took her hand and
squeezed. He wouldn't. Not so soon. Not now…

"Clara and I are getting married," he said clearly.

Sam let out a whoop and Angela gawped and Molly sat
back in her chair, stunned. Clara smiled weakly, wishing
she could throttle Ty. There was no backing out now, was
there? Just the way he wanted it. She looked at him and
saw a hint of apology in his eyes. Then he squeezed her
hand again and she felt a bit of her anger dissolve. What
was the point in waiting? It didn't change anything. And
time was ticking along.

"You're really getting married?" Molly asked, her eyes
wide.

Clara met her gaze and nodded. "Yes, we are."

"Oh, dear." And then Molly pushed back from the table,
came around the corner, and Clara got up to meet her.
Molly put her arms around her and hugged her for the
second time in an hour. "Thank you," she said, and Clara
heard tears in the older woman's voice. "It's just what I
wanted."

Clara started to laugh. Resistance was futile, wasn't
it? She loved this family. All the quirks, the dysfunction,
the love. She hugged Molly and then leaned back so she
could see her future mother-in-law's face. "We didn't really

plan it to be a birthday present," she said. "That comes later. With cake."

"Oh, presents be darned," Molly declared.

Ty looked at Clara. "Should we tell her, then?"

"Tell me what?" She let go of Clara and gave Ty the evil eye. "What are you up to, Tyson Diamond?"

Ty looked into Clara's eyes and gave her a slow smile, one that reached inside and took hold and made her want her own birthday cake so that she might close her eyes and blow out the candles and wish that this was all real and not just a forced, desperate decision. "I think you should," he urged.

Clara took a deep breath, gazed one more second in Ty's eyes, then took Molly's hands in hers. "Molly, remember that grandbaby you wished for?"

Molly's eyes grew even bigger as the words sank in. And Clara took one of the wrinkled hands and put it on her abdomen. "Happy birthday," she whispered.

"Oh," Molly breathed, and Clara saw tears form in Molly's eyes. "Oh, my. Oh." Her lip trembled. "I wish Virgil could be here for this. He would have been so happy. He always thought there was something special between you."

The words cut into Clara's soul just a bit; something special, yes, but it wasn't all it should be. She met Ty's gaze and she could see he was troubled, too, but then Molly kissed her cheek and Angela was hugging her gently and Ty rose to shake Sam's hand and get a clap on the back. "You've just bought us some time, brother," he said to Ty. Molly gave Sam's arm a swat as she went to hug Ty as well. Sam gave her an easy hug and smiled down at her. "This makes me Uncle Sam," he said, puffing out his chest.

Clara leaned in. "Don't get too cozy," she warned in an undertone. "When women see babies they get clucky.

And it wouldn't take much for your wife to get that glint in her eye."

At Sam's look of alarm she burst out laughing. Everyone took their seats again, and it seemed the cloud of uncertainty had lifted as people dug into their food.

She had a fork full of chow mein halfway to her mouth when she looked over at Ty and found him looking at her. He smiled.

It would be so easy to get used to this. To pretend it was all real. To want it to be real.

What had she done?

Ty put the overnight bag in the back seat and shut the door. Now that the weekend was over, Clara had to go back to Moose Jaw. She'd said yes and they'd told the family. It all seemed like a whirlwind of craziness. But as he held open the driver's side door for her, he couldn't stop the uncertainty that weighed heavily in his chest. He was terrified she'd change her mind the moment she was away from him. From Diamondback.

"I should get on the road," she reminded him.

He swallowed. Her breath made puffy clouds in the air and her eyes seemed unusually blue in the winter morning light. "Drive carefully and call me when you get there," he said. But he still didn't move to get out of the way so she could get behind the wheel.

"I will," she replied.

There had been a time yesterday—when she'd asked about love—that he'd considered confessing his feelings. He thought about it now, too. But he knew how it would look. Would she even believe him if he said it? He doubted it. He knew exactly how it would look—that he was saying it in reaction to the circumstances and not because he really meant it.

With Clara, he had to prove it. He knew the words were not enough. And he had to give her time. Because she'd had all the opportunity in the world to say the words yesterday, too—and she hadn't. In fact, she'd asked, "How can you be a real family without love?"

It wasn't the usual progression of things—baby, marriage, then love—but then nothing about his family followed the usual pattern. It didn't mean it couldn't work. He just had to take it slow. Their family depended on it.

"Clara, I…" He swore lightly. "Honestly, I think about everything I'm going to say about ten times before I say it."

She smiled. "Relax. I'm almost over being mad about yesterday."

He shifted uncomfortably. He hadn't exactly played it cool. And yet time was so short. Less than twenty-four hours later here she was, getting ready to leave. "I'm almost sorry about it," he replied, but he smiled back. "About the wedding, like I told you last night, whatever you want is fine."

"I thought about it. Something small, Ty. Just us and our families. And soon. I'd like for us to have some time to get settled before the baby turns things upside down." There was a sweet upturn to her lips. "I hear they do that."

"And I want to share the rest of the pregnancy with you, too," he added. "I want to be there for you from the start."

How much more plain could he be without actually saying the words?

She gasped and zipped open her purse, searching for something. A moment later she held up an envelope. "Here," she said. "I nearly forgot. I meant to give you this, but in all the commotion…" She handed it over.

"What is it?"

"Ultrasound pictures. I had them done last week. Everything's normal, but I'll have them done again in about six weeks."

Pictures. Of his child. He clutched the envelope in his hand.

"I've really got to go," she said. "I promise I'll call."

He moved aside and she climbed behind the wheel. He shut the door and listened as she started the engine, letting it warm for a few seconds before putting the car in reverse and turning it around on the parking pad. As she drove by him, she raised her fingers in farewell.

He stood in the driveway, watching until she turned on the road and out of sight. Then he opened the envelope and stared at the strange black-and-white film.

It would all work out. It had to.

CHAPTER TWELVE

Spring came early to Cadence Creek, and Ty and Clara's wedding day was unseasonably warm. Ty had heeded her request for a small wedding, but instead of her suggestion of the Diamondback living room, he'd convinced her to let him book the nearby bed-and-breakfast for the afternoon and night. Intimate and classy, Clara realized she was going to have a fairy-tale wedding after all—even if it was a scaled-down version.

She stood in the room they would share later, gazing at her figure in a cheval glass. She put her hand over her belly and the bump that was there now. Not just a bump but also the first little flutters of movement. Ty hadn't felt them yet, but she had. And each time it happened she thought of Ty, and Diamondback, and the future, and prayed that she was doing the right thing.

The fact that she still wasn't sure was troubling.

There was a knock on the door and she opened it to find Angela, Molly and Wendy standing with wide grins and white boxes. "The flowers are here," Wendy said. "And we wanted to see you before we go downstairs."

Molly and Wendy had hit it off immediately, and at the rehearsal dinner Clara had heard them promise to exchange quilting and knitting patterns. They were both thrilled about becoming grandmothers. And Ty had charmed the socks off his future mother-in-law. Now the two of them came into the suite in brand-new dresses and heels and matching smiles.

Angela took the lid off the first box. "This one is yours, Clara."

It was simple but stunning, a nosegay of red roses and baby's breath and white satin ribbon. Clara held it up and sniffed deeply. It all felt so surreal. After Jackson she'd never thought she'd get married. Never thought she'd have a family. And here she was, standing in a simple white dress with a bridal bouquet, and her matron of honor and two mothers looking on.

"Let's see yours," she said to Angela, and Angela took out the second bouquet—a smaller version of Clara's but all in white, contrasting with her deep red dress.

"You both look gorgeous," Wendy said.

Molly gave her a kiss on the cheek. "I'll second that. And I was going to wait until later to tell you, but I'm giving you and Ty the wedding ring quilt as a wedding present. You should have it. So many of the stitches are yours." She dabbed at her eyes. "You were part of the family long before today."

Clara fanned her eyes. "Oh, that's not fair! I just fixed my makeup." But she hugged Molly. "Thank you, Mom," she answered, and then there were sniffles on both sides.

Wendy gave Clara a final hug. "I'll see you downstairs. Love you, honey."

Clara blinked to keep from smudging her mascara. "You, too," she said, giving her a quick hug.

She'd worried about telling Wendy about moving back to Cadence Creek, but Wendy had been surprisingly supportive. "I lost you once before," she'd said. "Having you back in my life is the most important thing. Knowing I can visit you and the baby and knowing you can come visit us is enough."

And now the big day was here. Molly and Wendy left together and now it was just Angela and Clara left in the room. Angela arranged one of Clara's curls just right and stood back, admiring the dress. "You look amazing," she said. "When you said a short dress, I was skeptical, but it's perfect."

Clara ran a hand over the skirt, willing away the nerves that persisted in swirling in her stomach. The sheer cap sleeves were modest and feminine, and the skirt flowed to her knees where it flared slightly in a delicate, feminine ruffle. Tiny white satin heels completed the outfit, and her curls were frosted over by a simple short veil.

She was getting married.

To a man who didn't love her.

"Are you all right?" Angela asked. She took Clara's bouquet and put it on the bed. "You got pale all of a sudden."

Clara smiled weakly. "This has all happened so fast," she confessed. "I just need a minute to get my bearings."

"Oh, honey." Angela led her to the bed and they sat down. "Are you sure this is what you want? You went from telling Ty to being engaged all in a weekend, and here you are barely a month later getting married."

"I love him," she said to Angela, and despite her mascara fears, two tears slipped over her lids and down her cheek.

"Well, I'm relieved to hear that," Angela said, her voice thick as she reached for a tissue from the box beside the bed. "Isn't it a good thing?"

"But it's not why he's marrying me," she answered. "It's all because of the baby. And because he is so determined to do the right thing by our child that he said he'd leave the ranch behind to be with us. How could I ask him to do that? He was willing to give up so much for us. And I love it here. It would be selfish."

Angela rubbed her arm.

"I just don't know how to do this and still keep my heart intact."

Angela wiped her eyes and blew her nose. "Ty is the most honorable man I know—with one obvious exception," Angela said. "He wouldn't have asked you to marry him if he didn't have feelings for you."

Clara didn't know how to explain it any further. Feelings were not the same thing as love. It was hard to build a life on "feelings." It was hard to trust your heart to feelings. And expressing her doubt made her feel ungrateful and selfish.

"I'll be fine," she assured Angela. "It's just last-minute jitters."

There was a discreet knock on the door. It was time.

"Here." Angela dabbed beneath Clara's eyes. "That's better." She picked up her bouquet and handed Clara hers. "All set?"

"As ready as I'm going to be," Clara answered.

Ty waited in the parlor, locking and unlocking his knee nervously. A small fire blazed in the fireplace behind him; he could feel the heat against the back of his legs. The minister stood beside him, and the handful of guests sat in chairs brought in from the dining room for the occasion. There was the smell of roses in the air and Ty heard a small knock and then a door opening and shutting.

It was really happening.

Sam put a reassuring hand on his shoulder. "Breathe," he instructed.

Angela appeared in the door, stepping slowly and smil-

ing at Sam in a way that made Ty's heart clench. She
stepped to the side and then there was Clara, standing in
the doorway, her fingers clutching her bouquet.

My God, she was beautiful. Catch-your-breath beautiful, in a floaty white dress and filmy veil over her hair. He
smiled, but the smile slipped as he saw her face go white
and her teeth worried her lip.

She always did that when she was afraid and unsure.
Cold panic ran like ice water through his veins as he saw
the wild look in her eyes—a split second before she turned
on her heel and disappeared.

Angela took a step to go after her, but Ty stalled her
with a hand. "No," he said. "I did this. It has to be me."

It was hard to breathe. The breaths were coming short
and fast and Clara felt slightly lightheaded from it all. She
stumbled through the back door of the B and B into what
would, in the summer, be a back garden for afternoon tea
or an al fresco breakfast. Right now it was slightly soggy
and brown with a few brave spears of new grass poking
through. She dropped her flowers in a dry bird bath and
rested her hands on the cool concrete edge. She had to
breathe.

"Clara!"

The screen door slammed with a bang and she heard
his footsteps behind her. Humiliation burned through her.
She should have put a stop to this from the beginning. It
never should have gone this far.

"Clara," he said, quieter now, gently. "Breathe, honey.
It's all right."

She hated that his soothing tone worked. Hated that
she'd come to rely on him this much, hated that she loved
him so much that the thought of marrying him when
that emotion wasn't returned was too much to bear. She

couldn't look him in the eye. And she had no idea what to do next. There was just a bunch of nothingness stretched out before her. Clara, who was always able to see one step ahead, even when times were at their worst, had ground to a complete standstill.

"It's okay," he said, still not touching her with anything but his voice. "I shouldn't have pushed so hard. I thought…" He stopped, cleared his throat. "I don't want you to marry me if you don't love me, Clara. I should have listened to you. We can figure the rest out, I promise. I'll be the best father I can. But I won't ask you to go into a marriage with a man you don't love. I was wrong to do that."

Her fingers tightened on the bird bath. It was the only thing holding her upright. Had he just said… But it made no sense! Was he saying he was in love with her? But that wasn't exactly what he'd said, was it? Only that he wouldn't pressure her to go into a marriage if *she* didn't love *him*.

"What about you?" she finally asked, closing her eyes. "You were willing to marry a woman you didn't love. And you didn't back out, did you? You were going to see it through." Her voice caught on a sob. "I don't know what's wrong with me, Ty!"

"Who said I was marrying a woman I didn't love?"

The words echoed through the bare garden for a heart-stopping moment. Slowly she turned to face him. Her heart started beating again, a little too fast. He was so dashing in his suit and serious eyes and unsmiling lips. He was a man filled with purpose, she realized. And that purpose was her. Joy pierced her like a shining beam of sunlight.

"You love me?"

"I do. I have for some time. Maybe from the first moment I took you in my arms and danced with you at Sam and Angela's wedding, but I was too stupid to realize it. But I've known for sure since the night you told me you were pregnant."

Her mind spun back to everything that happened that weekend. Everything that had been said. "Why didn't you tell me?" she wailed. "It would have made things so much easier!"

"Because," he said, coming closer. "You would have thought I was only saying it because of the baby. You would have wondered if it was true or if I was trying to manipulate you into getting my way." Another step. "And because I knew you didn't feel the same way about me and I wasn't willing to put myself out there like that."

"Didn't feel the same way?" Clara let her fingers release the bird bath and faced him full-on. "Tyson. I have loved you since the night you kissed me under the stars. You made me believe in *me* again. You made me feel whole again. Do you think I could have made love with you otherwise?"

He took the final step and gathered her in his arms, lifting her until her toes barely touched the hard ground. "Thank God," he said close to her ear. "I didn't know I could even fall in love. And I certainly didn't know if anyone could fall in love with me."

"Because you never showed anyone who you really are. But I saw it. And that's the man I fell in love with. I was just too scared to admit it. To let myself be that vulnerable again. To trust anyone and give them the power to hurt me."

He put her back down on the ground but kept his arms around her. "Do you trust me now?"

She nodded. "Everything you've done has been to try to do the right thing. If I'd been smart, I would have seen with my eyes what you didn't say. I guess we're both a couple of blind fools."

"Not anymore."

"No, not anymore. I used to have a saying, did you know that? 'Living in fear is not living.' But that's exactly what I was doing. I was so afraid to love you." She cuddled into him, drawing strength from him just as she'd always done. "I was wrong about that."

He stepped back a little and held her fingers in his. "So, are we going to do this thing? Because I'd sure like to marry you today, Clara Ferguson. Marry you and make us a family."

"I'd like that." This time her smile was free and it felt glorious. "I'd like that a lot."

"I love you," he declared. "Just to be perfectly clear."

"And I love you. Let's get married."

He grabbed her roses from the bird bath, put them in her hands, and she gave a delighted little laugh as he swung her up in his arms and carried her over the threshold to a brand-new life.

EPILOGUE

CLARA TUCKED THE tiny feet into frilly bottoms and buttoned the row of tiny buttons up the front of the pink-and-white dress, quite efficiently when all flailing legs and arms were considered. She laughed as she lifted baby Susanna into her arms. Today was a special day and deserved a fancy dress. It wasn't every day that Uncle Sam and Aunt Angela celebrated an anniversary.

Molly tiptoed into the nursery. "Is the coast clear?"

Clara laughed. "Oh, she's bright eyed and bushy tailed. No need to tread softly. I think this is a girl ready for a party. Come on, Susanna Banana."

"Come to Grandma," Molly crooned, and took the infant from Clara's arms. "There's my girl." She looked up at Clara. "My, Virgil would have loved her."

"I wish he could have been here," Clara agreed, smoothing the back of the dress and smiling. "But I think he's probably somewhere feeling very satisfied about the part he played in bringing this all together."

"I think you're right. Okay, little one, there's a party happening around here. Let's get some cake."

Ty was coming through the deck doors with a platter of steaks, and Angela was in the kitchen putting together a salad. Sam had given Buster a bone and put him in the back yard to gnaw to his heart's content.

Her family.

Ty came over and planted a kiss on her lips while Molly perched on a chair and bounced Susanna on her knee, saying a silly rhyme. But when dinner was ready, they all gathered around the table for a celebratory toast. Clara did the honors of popping the champagne she'd bought especially for the occasion, and she filled five glasses, handing them around.

This time Ty did the honors. "Happy anniversary, to my brother and the woman brave enough to put up with him."

"Ty!" Clara exclaimed, but everyone laughed and tilted their glasses. Except Angela...

Molly's eagle eye noticed. "Something wrong with the champagne?"

Angela met Sam's gaze and they shared a tender glance before she turned back to Molly. "Well, Ty and Clara got the birthday announcement. We figured we'd save it for the anniversary." She put down her glass and put her fingers over her belly. "Is it too soon for another grandchild?"

"Never!" Molly jumped up and hugged Angela tightly until Susanna began to fuss and complain. She lifted the baby and her grin was from ear to ear.

"You are going to have a cousin," she announced. Then she looked at Sam and Ty. "Cousins," she remarked, "as close as siblings."

Tucking the baby on her arm, she raised her glass and took a healthy sip. "Ah," she said. "Is there anything better than family?"

There really wasn't.

* * * * *

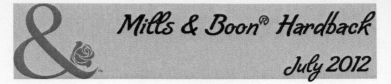

Mills & Boon® Hardback
July 2012

ROMANCE

The Secrets She Carried	Lynne Graham
To Love, Honour and Betray	Jennie Lucas
Heart of a Desert Warrior	Lucy Monroe
Unnoticed and Untouched	Lynn Raye Harris
A Royal World Apart	Maisey Yates
Distracted by her Virtue	Maggie Cox
The Count's Prize	Christina Hollis
The Tarnished Jewel of Jazaar	Susanna Carr
Keeping Her Up All Night	Anna Cleary
The Rules of Engagement	Ally Blake
Argentinian in the Outback	Margaret Way
The Sheriff's Doorstep Baby	Teresa Carpenter
The Sheikh's Jewel	Melissa James
The Rebel Rancher	Donna Alward
Always the Best Man	Fiona Harper
How the Playboy Got Serious	Shirley Jump
Sydney Harbour Hospital: Marco's Temptation	Fiona McArthur
Dr Tall, Dark...and Dangerous?	Lynne Marshall

MEDICAL

The Legendary Playboy Surgeon	Alison Roberts
Falling for Her Impossible Boss	Alison Roberts
Letting Go With Dr Rodriguez	Fiona Lowe
Waking Up With His Runaway Bride	Louisa George

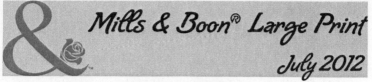

ROMANCE

Roccanti's Marriage Revenge	Lynne Graham
The Devil and Miss Jones	Kate Walker
Sheikh Without a Heart	Sandra Marton
Savas's Wildcat	Anne McAllister
A Bride for the Island Prince	Rebecca Winters
The Nanny and the Boss's Twins	Barbara McMahon
Once a Cowboy...	Patricia Thayer
When Chocolate Is Not Enough...	Nina Harrington

HISTORICAL

The Mysterious Lord Marlowe	Anne Herries
Marrying the Royal Marine	Carla Kelly
A Most Unladylike Adventure	Elizabeth Beacon
Seduced by Her Highland Warrior	Michelle Willingham

MEDICAL

The Boss She Can't Resist	Lucy Clark
Heart Surgeon, Hero...Husband?	Susan Carlisle
Dr Langley: Protector or Playboy?	Joanna Neil
Daredevil and Dr Kate	Leah Martyn
Spring Proposal in Swallowbrook	Abigail Gordon
Doctor's Guide to Dating in the Jungle	Tina Beckett

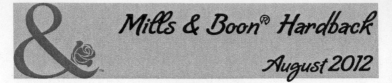

ROMANCE

Contract with Consequences	Miranda Lee
The Sheikh's Last Gamble	Trish Morey
The Man She Shouldn't Crave	Lucy Ellis
The Girl He'd Overlooked	Cathy Williams
A Tainted Beauty	Sharon Kendrick
One Night With The Enemy	Abby Green
The Dangerous Jacob Wilde	Sandra Marton
His Last Chance at Redemption	Michelle Conder
The Hidden Heart of Rico Rossi	Kate Hardy
Marrying the Enemy	Nicola Marsh
Mr Right, Next Door!	Barbara Wallace
The Cowboy Comes Home	Patricia Thayer
The Rancher's Housekeeper	Rebecca Winters
Her Outback Rescuer	Marion Lennox
Monsoon Wedding Fever	Shoma Narayanan
If the Ring Fits...	Jackie Braun
Sydney Harbour Hospital: Ava's Re-Awakening	Carol Marinelli
How To Mend A Broken Heart	Amy Andrews

MEDICAL

Falling for Dr Fearless	Lucy Clark
The Nurse He Shouldn't Notice	Susan Carlisle
Every Boy's Dream Dad	Sue MacKay
Return of the Rebel Surgeon	Connie Cox

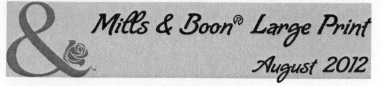

Mills & Boon® Large Print

August 2012

ROMANCE

A Deal at the Altar — Lynne Graham
Return of the Moralis Wife — Jacqueline Baird
Gianni's Pride — Kim Lawrence
Undone by His Touch — Annie West
The Cattle King's Bride — Margaret Way
New York's Finest Rebel — Trish Wylie
The Man Who Saw Her Beauty — Michelle Douglas
The Last Real Cowboy — Donna Alward
The Legend of de Marco — Abby Green
Stepping out of the Shadows — Robyn Donald
Deserving of His Diamonds? — Melanie Milburne

HISTORICAL

The Scandalous Lord Lanchester — Anne Herries
Highland Rogue, London Miss — Margaret Moore
His Compromised Countess — Deborah Hale
The Dragon and the Pearl — Jeannie Lin
Destitute On His Doorstep — Helen Dickson

MEDICAL

Sydney Harbour Hospital: Lily's Scandal — Marion Lennox
Sydney Harbour Hospital: Zoe's Baby — Alison Roberts
Gina's Little Secret — Jennifer Taylor
Taming the Lone Doc's Heart — Lucy Clark
The Runaway Nurse — Dianne Drake
The Baby Who Saved Dr Cynical — Connie Cox

0712 GEN STD LP